Winner
Jabuti Award for Book of the Year
(2016)

Winner
Oceanos Prize for Literature in Portuguese
(2016)

Winner
José Saramago Literary Prize
(2017)

Winner
Anna Seghers Prize
(2018)

RESISTANCE

CHARCO PRESS

First published by Charco Press 2018

Charco Press Ltd., Office 59, 44–46 Morningside Road, Edinburgh EH10 4BF

A CIP catalogue record for this book is available from the British Library.

ISBN: 9781999859329
e-book: 9781999859374

www.charcopress.com

Edited by Annie McDermott
Cover design by Pablo Font
Typeset by Laura Jones

This book has been selected to receive financial assistance from English PEN's 'PEN Translates' programme, supported by Arts Council England. English PEN exists to promote literature and our understanding of it, to uphold writers' freedoms around the world, to campaign against the persecution and imprisonment of writers for stating their views, and to promote the friendly cooperation of writers and the free exchange of ideas.
www.englishpen.org

2 4 6 8 10 9 7 5 3

Supported using public funding by
ARTS COUNCIL ENGLAND

ENGLISH PEN

LOTTERY FUNDED

Julián Fuks

RESISTANCE

Translated by
Daniel Hahn

CHARCO PRESS

For Emi, much more than a possible brother

I think it's important to resist: that's been my motto.
But today, how often have I asked myself
how best to embody that word.

Ernesto Sábato

1.

My brother is adopted, but I can't say and don't want to say that my brother is adopted. If I say this, if I speak these words that I have long taken care to silence, I reduce my brother to a single categorical condition, a single essential attribute: my brother is something, and this something is what so many people try to see in him, this something is the set of marks we insist on looking for, despite ourselves, in his features, in his gestures, in his acts. My brother is adopted, but I don't want to reinforce the stigma that the word evokes, the stigma that is the word itself made character. I don't want to deepen his scar, and if I don't want to do this, I must not say scar.

I could use the verb in the past tense and say my brother was adopted, thereby freeing him from that eternal present, from perpetuity, but I can't get over the strangeness of this formulation. My brother wasn't some different thing until he was adopted; my brother became my brother the moment he was adopted, or rather, the moment I was born, some years later. If I say my brother was adopted, it's as though I were reporting quite calmly that I'd lost him, that he was kidnapped, that I had a brother until somebody came and took him far away.

The remaining option is the most sayable; of all the possibilities, it's the one that causes the least disquiet, or that best disguises it. My brother is an adoptive son.

There's something technical about the term, adoptive son, which contributes to its social acceptability. There's a novelty to it that absolves him, just for an instant, of the blemishes of the past, that seems to cleanse him of any undesirable meanings. I say my brother is an adoptive son and people nod solemnly, masking any sorrow, lowering their eyes as though they weren't eager to ask anything more. Perhaps they share my uneasiness, or perhaps they really do forget the whole business with the next sip or the next forkful. If the uneasiness continues to reverberate within me, it's because I also hear this phrase partially — my brother is a son — and it's hard to accept that it won't end up leading to the usual tautological truth: my brother is the son of my parents. I chant over and over that my brother is a son and the question always springs to my lips: whose son?

2.

I don't want to imagine an icy, gloomy, cavernous space, a silence made even more severe by the muteness of a skinny baby boy. I don't want to imagine the strong hand that grabs him by the calves, the harsh slaps that don't stop until you hear him crying in distress. I don't want to imagine the shrillness of that crying, the desperation of the little boy drawing his first breath, longing for the arms of someone ready to receive him – arms he will not be granted. I don't want to imagine a mother in agony, reaching out, one more sob muffled by the rumble of boots against the floor, boots that leave and take him with them: the child vanishes and what remains is the size of the room, what remains is the emptiness. I don't want to imagine a son as a woman fallen. I prefer to let these images dissipate into the unheard-of world of nightmares, nightmares that inhabit me or that once inhabited a bed beside my own.

I wouldn't know how to describe a happy childbirth. A white room, white sheets, and white for the gloves that receive the child, too, white and plastic, impersonal, scientific. No happiness, certainly, in the total asepsis. An obstetrician who takes him into his neutral hands and examines him: the child is intact, the child is breathing, his skin rosy, the flexing of his limbs is good, heart rate regular. Best for his mother not to see him, or rather, for the woman who gave birth to him not to see him. No point in the potential confusion of feelings, especially at such a susceptible moment, the pain of the labour fading, a weight being lifted, perhaps a slight sense of emptiness. Nothing to be gained from uncertainty like that. Being held in provisional arms will be of no benefit to him; better for him to meet his real parents as soon as possible, when they are open-armed and ready to receive him, eager and certain, for a full welcome.

Let me be honest with myself: I would rather not become too absorbed in the images of this birth. To tell of a child being born is to tell of a sudden existence, of somebody coming into being, and that moment doesn't matter to anyone as much as it does to the child who is bursting into life. To bestow upon this birth the appropriate tone of joy, the tone I'd like it to deserve, that I'd like my brother to deserve just as all life deserves it, I would have to appeal to the smiles of those who would very soon find themselves before him, those who would at last be ready to call him son. They must have been wide, those smiles, a suitable fading of the nerves that comes with any longed-for relief. But a child is not born to bring relief, he is born and as soon as he is born he demands relief himself. A child doesn't cry in order to enable a smile in others; he cries so that they pick him up, and protect him, and with their caresses soothe the implacable feeling of helplessness that has already begun to torment him. I don't want to imagine a boy as the downfall of a woman, nor can I imagine him as the salvation of another family, of the family that would later be mine, an unreasonable salvation they should never have asked of him.

3.

He's adopted, that's what I once said to a cousin when she insisted on pointing out how different we were, he and I, his hair darker and curlier than mine, his eyes so much lighter. I don't think there was any malice or spite in my statement, I must have been about five years old – though if I now feel compelled to defend myself, perhaps I really was seized by some innocent cruelty which to this day I am still seeking to conceal. We were in a car being driven by my father, and my mother couldn't have been with us because my brother was in the front seat, perhaps following our conversation, or perhaps lost in his own unfathomable thoughts. In an instant, there was silence. I might have been elbowed discreetly by my sister, who I imagine sitting beside me, or maybe the jab was merely the discomfort I felt upon realising I'd done something wrong, a discomfort I so often felt without anyone needing to elbow me. So bruising was the silence that I remember it to this day, among so many other silences that I can barely remember.

I'm not trying to absolve myself for my mistake when I say that in those days the guidance we received was ambiguous and vague. My brother had always known he was adopted, that was what my parents said, and it had always intrigued me, or intrigues me now: how to say something on that scale to a child who can barely manage the simplest words, how coldly or distantly to pronounce mummy, daddy, baby, adoption. How to convey the importance of that fact, with the seriousness the subject demands, without assigning it unnecessary weight, without transforming it into a burden the boy will never be able to carry? It was Winnicott who was dictating the steps we took – we followed a lot of what was suggested by Winnicottian theory, that's what I would hear many years later, not quite understanding the term but aware of the plaintive tone, the distress in the voice. The fact of his knowing, of our knowing, of everyone who lived in the house knowing, was itself basic knowledge. And yet, somehow, this process was then put into reverse, a time coming when what had once been a word became unsayable, the truth silenced as though that might make it disappear. I don't think it's inaccurate to say that it was my brother who imposed on all of us the silence he found most comfortable, and we simply accepted it, so kind, and so cowardly.

In my memory, my brother's eyes were filled with tears, but I suspect this is an invented detail, added later, on one of the first times I recalled the episode, already clouded by a certain remorse. He was sitting in the front seat. If he was crying, he certainly held back any sobs and hid his tears with his hands, or he turned his face to the window, let his eyes drift over presumed pedestrians. The point is, he wouldn't look at me, he wouldn't turn around. Maybe they were mine, those tear-filled eyes.

4.

How strong is silence when it stretches well beyond the immediate discomfort, well beyond the hurt. For years I've noticed, impressed, how my brother can quickly dismiss any thoughts that displease him, interrupt conversations without seeming abrupt, change the subject without even noticing, slip between one idea and another in a way that's almost instantaneous, seamless. I see his face crumple for just a moment at some vague misfortune, some unhappy words that nobody ended up saying, a minuscule hint of or approach towards what's bothering him, only to return to his normal expression, his indifference, his anaesthetised neutrality. There is no shortage of clues to suggest he has managed to forget, though forget isn't quite the right word − repress is what my parents would say here, I can tell. There's no shortage of evidence that he spends long periods without admitting it even to himself, without accepting or recognising it − days, months, maybe years, locked away in his room without any of this overwhelming him, without his mind being revisited by everything that I don't want to say and cannot say, everything that I need to say. And has he no need to say it to himself?

How strong is silence when it stretches well beyond, I ask myself, well beyond the immediate discomfort, and the hurt, but also well beyond blame, and finally I come to my answer. I too, for a long time, have been able to forget. We are in the car again, now it's a long journey and the tiredness is affecting us almost as much as the boredom, the heat, the frustration, and here once again I seem to be trying to justify my callousness, my foolishness. For some reason I'm annoyed at my sister, I don't want to be sitting next to her any more, sharing the space and the journey with her, but I'm forced to and this makes me desperate: I'm not your brother. I announce that I am not her brother and she gets indignant, you can't do that, you are my brother, that's just how it is, you're my brother and you're going to be my brother forever. I insist, I don't want to, you're not my sister and that's that, it's decided, I've decided. She appeals to my father, who acknowledges quite reasonably that she's in the right, stifling a laugh, and my mother agrees and she laughs too, amused at the absurdity of it all, at the extent of my stubbornness. No verdict means anything to me at that moment: I don't care, to hell with you all, I'm not her brother and that's that.

The anecdote has become a family classic, repeated over dinner even when all those present have heard it before, as a general example of childish folly or as proof of my excessive obstinacy. It's always recounted in the cheerful tone that the two of them in front, my parents, assign to it. Two of us who were sitting in the back also take on this same tone, we also remember the episode as something funny, even seeing it as contributing to the complicity that we managed to establish between us.

But there were five of us in the car. My brother didn't comment, and he still doesn't today, preferring to stay silent at his corner of the table, simply swallowing what's left of his meal, withdrawing earlier and earlier. I was sitting in the middle, between my sister and him, and I must have turned my back on him as I argued, doing my best to defend my impossible position. I don't know how this effort of mine must have sounded to his ears, if he was pleased to hear how little I valued blood ties, or if it was painful to hear how precariously I treated fraternal bonds. I didn't question whether he was my brother, our relationship was not something I wanted to disrupt. But I wonder whether he didn't, all the same, just for a moment, frown, lower his eyes, his little boy's face crumpling.

5.

I walk the streets of Buenos Aires, and look at people's faces. I wrote a whole book based on my experience of walking the streets of Buenos Aires and looking at people's faces. I wanted them to act as my mirror, to replicate me on every corner, I wanted to discover I was Argentinian by my simple aptitude for camouflage, so that I might finally walk among equals. I never thought what it would be like for my brother to walk the streets of Buenos Aires. The uncertain anxiety that would run up his spine at every recognisable feature, every common gesture, every lingering stare, every familiar-looking face. The immense fear – or expectation – that someday a face would show itself to be his mirror, that somebody just the same really might appear in front of him, and that this same person might be replicated into so many more.

I suddenly understand, or want to understand, why my brother stopped spending time in this city that we never managed to quit. Buenos Aires is where my parents were forced to leave when he was not yet six months old, Buenos Aires is what we all felt jettisoned from as long as they weren't allowed back – even if some of us, my sister and I, had never even set our tiny feet on its pavements. Can exile be inherited? Might we, the little ones, be as expatriate as our parents? Should we consider ourselves Argentinians deprived of our country, of our fatherland? And is political persecution subject to the norms of heredity? These questions did not arise for my brother: he didn't depend on our parents to be Argentinian, to be exiled, to have been deprived of the land of his birth. Perhaps that was something we envied, the autonomy of his identity, the way he didn't need to struggle so hard for his Argentinianness. He had been born there, he was more Argentinian than us, he always would be more Argentinian than us, however little that might mean. Which is why we were surprised, years later, when he stopped accompanying us on our insistent visits to the city, for the long periods in which we tried to recover the something that had, indirectly, perhaps, been stolen from us.

I walk the streets of Buenos Aires and I stop at the Plaza del Congreso, outside the headquarters of the Mothers of the Plaza de Mayo. I hesitate a moment at the door, I can't make up my mind to go in. I've been there on other occasions just as a tourist or out of curiosity, I've run my eyes over every shelf in the bookstore, I've had a coffee in the gallery, I've let myself be imbued with its testimonials, its stories, its slogans. Now I realise I don't want to go in, that I'm standing at the door and I don't want to be standing at the door. That I'm standing at the door because I wish my brother were here in my place.

6.

Wh hat did we do on those countless nights when we shared a bedroom? Who fell asleep first, consigning the other to silence and uninhabitable darkness, to the fear of the shadows, to the shock of each creak? What erratic reveries would seize the one left behind, what childish ghosts would haunt him, while his brother snored calmly, indifferent and pitiless? Who asked the other if he was asleep yet, just so the concreteness of his shaky voice might fill the inscrutable space that separated them?

These questions are fallacious, too lyrical to contain any truth. By choosing to tell this story through its night-time terrors, I'm placing myself at the centre of the anguish, I'm making myself the protagonist, I'm assigning contempt unfairly to my brother. I was the one who resisted sleeping with the light off, I was the one who got up scared in the middle of the night, went down the gloomy corridor and sought refuge in my parents' bed. Sometimes, in the small hours of the morning, my sister would also be taken into that spacious double bed, and there we slept on, together, squashed up, four-fifths of the family confined to a few square metres. My brother remained apart, between his own sheets, and the solitude that embraced him must have been deeper, even if the tranquillity he didn't fear was not.

This story might be very different if I could actually remember it. For eight years I lived in the same bedroom as my brother, in the same series of bedrooms, and I can't remember how we talked, if we had fun, if we played some common game or got into some argument or other that did away with any age difference, if he taught me his childish mischiefs without my having to suffer from them myself. Maybe not, maybe we kept our distance, maybe we intimidated each other and bored each other with the same emptiness that consumes us, sometimes, today.

I remember the geography of the rooms, the position of the bed, the other bed, the wardrobe, the desk by the window that loosed us into the vastness of the city, be that São Paulo or Buenos Aires. I remember the bright posters he used to stick on the walls, perhaps hoping I might share his enthusiasms. I remember a few toys of mine, inane pieces of plastic that fascinated me, dolls I used to involve in complex narratives all morning long, all afternoon long, tirelessly, until he came back. The imagination in those days was a fertile thing, a fruitful fiction that has abandoned me now. I can't remember what it was like spending a minute, ten minutes, an hour by his side, and I can't make it up either. How eight years can have gone by like that is a question I can't answer, yet another conception of reality being avoided here.

I know he protected me, and not because my mother insists on boasting about it, emphasising how much he loved me, her covert way of begging me to go and knock on his door one more time. I know he protected me because one customary gesture of his sticks in my memory: his hand resting on the back of my neck, his index finger and thumb pressing onto the skin on either side, each in turn, not too hard, just indicating the direction of the next step. That was how he led me when we walked side by side, in the middle of any crowd that happened to surround us.

7.

This is not just a story, not just his story. This is history.

This is history, and yet, almost everything I have at my disposal is memory, fleeting notions of days long gone, impressions that precede consciousness and language, destitute relics I insist on embezzling into words. This isn't a matter of some abstract preoccupation, though I do make use of abstractions: I've looked for my brother in what little I've written up to now and he is nowhere to be found. Maybe some idea would have done him justice, the description might by chance have evoked him, the handful of apparently truthful facts I've spread into my winding paragraphs, but nothing. From this unnecessary observation, you are not to assume naïveté on my part, at least not for now: I'm well aware that no book could encapsulate any human being, no book could ever reconstruct in paper and ink an existence of blood and flesh. What I'm saying here is something more serious, not just a kind of literary formalism: I'm talking about the fear of losing my brother, and I feel with every sentence that I'm losing him more.

For a moment I'm confused, I forget that things can also precede words, that trying to tap into them will always involve new fallacies, and I go around this apartment just as I went around the text, in search of traces of my brother, something that might restore his reality to me. I'm not in his house, my parents' house, where I can imagine him shut up in the bedroom, I can't knock on his door. There are thousands of kilometres separating us, a whole country separating us, but one thing that works to my advantage is our mother's strange habit of scattering the family homes with objects that keep us in contact. This Buenos Aires apartment has nobody living in it. Ever since my grandparents' death it's just been a place for passing through, a crossroads for distant relatives, distracted and hurried, who have forgotten one another's existence. I happen upon a photo album lying flat on the bookcase, left at just the perfect angle to look casual. I have to turn a few pages before I'm finally assailed by my brother's face, before I'm finally surprised by what I was already expecting.

The photo doesn't say what I want it to say, the photo doesn't say anything. The photo is merely his soft face in the middle of a shady veranda, his eyes looking at me through the photographer's lens, those eyes that are so light, that hair smoother than I could have imagined – his childish beauty that perhaps I envied. His head is tilted to one side as though he were asking something, but I know it's not for me to make up what it is. His half-open lips are quiet, too, but that's where my gaze is drawn merely to be quite sure of the injustice I am doing him, the injustice I'm doing my brother in this very indelicate attempt. I can't make this boy, the boy and the man he is today, a fragile character. I can't assign some unreasonable pain or other to him, reducing him to an excessive sensitivity that might evoke pity, subjecting him to easy distress. And above all, I cannot make my brother mute, deprived of any means of defending himself, of confessing himself – or of keeping quiet when the situation calls for it. Why can I not let him speak, attribute even the smallest phrase to him in this fiction? With this book will I be trying to steal his life, to steal his image, and also to steal, in minor thefts, his silence and his voice?

I can't decide if this is a story.

8.

When you're one of three children, being one of three children is enough and you're already creating a multiple universe of complicities, exclusions and alliances. A game I might be retrieving intact from some secret corner of memory or I might just be inventing now, assigning roles like the person in charge, redeeming my own inaction with words. I can see, or invent, my brother summoning us silently, holding a finger to his lips: he wants us to gather all the cushions, pillows, mattresses we can carry without being seen, and pile everything up in the corridor, dividing the apartment into two halves. He wants us to build a great barricade together, not yet knowing, not even suspecting, that the great barricade will divide us, too.

Those were good moments, when we threw ourselves against that soft barrier, trying to clear the top in acrobatic leaps, committed only to impulsiveness, the inconsequence of bodies. We were siblings, and being siblings made it easier to appreciate the irresponsibility, to fantasise about an unlikely accusation by the adults, their censuring of the risks we were supposedly taking. In my brother's jumps those risks became spectacular, and it wasn't unusual for me and my sister to step aside just to watch, full of wonder at his skill, amazement at his courage. Some would say this was his way of dispelling his aggression, that by throwing himself into the void he was mastering his anguish and helplessness – the anguish that was reflected in our eyes and that we too dissipated merely by watching him. But none of that seemed to cloud the joy of those acts, none of that made the smile fade from his face, a smile that was so uncommon in him.

It wouldn't be long before the smile would fade, as the game threatened to come to an end. We were siblings, and among siblings any coalition is temporary, any peace is fleeting, any sign of affection heralds the next inevitable attack, which might be brought on by the mildest word. At the first command I would find myself beside my brother, on one side of the barricade, cushions quickly piled up, and then battle would commence. My sister was now the enemy to be subdued, my sister who would soon give up on any counterpunches, bending beneath the dense hailstorm, lying face-down and shielding the back of her neck with her forearms. My sister's curled-up body like a silhouette drawn on the ground – can I see that image or am I making it up? Do I add my puny blows to my brother's or do I in that moment manage to defy him, to break our pact, to become my brother's brother and denounce the cowardly acts being perpetrated there?

That night we waited in silence for our sister's return, we waited at the kitchen table, by the door, wanting to be there when she arrived. When she arrived she was still inconsolable, she was still sobbing, and my father's expression was stern. The front tooth that had been cracked would never be perfectly repaired, that was what the dentist herself had said: now it was half resin, and the colour of the tooth and the colour of the resin would never be the same. I don't know how we reacted, my brother and I, if there was any anguish our eyes could express, any kind of sympathy, any polite pity. I think I wanted to sleep in her room, just for that night, but I was too ashamed to say so.

9.

I sit at the dining-room table, even though I'm alone. Sitting at the table, not hungry, without any dinner, I feel as if there are many silences accompanying me, I feel as though every absence is demanding its place. It's nine p.m. in Buenos Aires, nine p.m. in São Paulo: in that other room my parents must be sitting at the table, some leftovers on the plates that they've carefully pushed aside, no new subjects to discuss, no new yearnings to confess, each of them drawing circles in their teacup. My hands rest on the desolate surface: I notice that I too am drawing shapes with the tip of a finger, following a furrow in the wood, but the furrow doesn't make a complete circle and my movement is pendular. By now, my brother must already have gone back to his room, that's as much as I can imagine. He swallowed some of what they served him as best he could, bestowed his usual monosyllables upon them, and then got up and left without a sound, failing to reply to what they failed to ask.

I don't know where he would have been sitting, I don't know where they sit when I'm not there. My father is always at the head, my mother to his right, but opposite her, to his left, in the spot where ancient custom would place the firstborn, none of us ever managed to establish ourselves. For years, my brother seemed to accept this as his natural place, fitting into an unsuspected hierarchy

21

that nobody needed to articulate. My sister and I would choose from the other chairs according to some private logic – following the gender distinction already in place, as far as I can guess, her aligned with my mother, me with my brother. It was only later that he started hanging around in his room for longer, ignoring the insistent calls that we took it in turn to yell, ever more vehement calls that only ended up spoiling his mood. We couldn't even hear his voice when he finally surrendered to dinner, his eyes then were a sad curtain of eyelids, but so comprehensive was his withdrawal, so resonant his silence, that he seemed to occupy the whole space and compel us to fall silent, too. I think it was just to avoid this small daily battle that we started to occupy his chair, my sister or I, whoever was first troubled by the emptiness that opened up between us, whoever first dared to break with tradition. In the years that followed, the firstborn was no longer whoever had arrived first into the world, but whoever arrived first at the table and dared to establish themselves there.

He would leave before dessert, I think he always left before dessert, and I'm not referring here to the usual meagre fruit that we never tired of, whatever Argentinian fruit could be found in São Paulo, or to the measured-out portions of chocolate that would grow progressively as our bodies grew. I'm referring to dessert as it's conceived of in the Spanish-speaking world, the time spent at the table after all hunger has been sated, a time for retrieving in words a past that refuses to recede into the distance, a chance to scrutinise life in its many banal details. Why was there such attachment to the past, why did we keep trotting out the old days in all those aimless stories, it was a question that none of us asked, one of the many inquiries we failed to make. Tonight I think I understand why my parents never found an answer. If I sit at the table at nine o'clock, without any dinner, not hungry, if tonight my solitude takes the shape of those four vacant chairs, it's because I wish I could, just one more time, hear those stories.

10.

It was always assumed that the story began in Germany, but if the family was Jewish, and even if it wasn't, if the family existed since times unimaginable just like every family exists, all deriving from the same distant absolute forefather, then it's obvious that this beginning was arbitrarily defined and that it could have come at any time, in any ancient place inhabited by human beings. It was assumed that the story began in Germany because that's where our name came from, and also because there, in a still-mythical genealogy, one of our ancestors had been the father of botany – earning himself a flower and a colour that make reference to his name, a flower and a colour that we have also inherited. But these were incidental and somewhat irrelevant details. The true story of that half of the family started much later, among those who headed for Romania, buying land in Transylvania and adapting their writing to their new language. In some unrecorded village, then, the grandfather I never knew was born, an Abraham of legend, not very far from where my grandmother was born, one Ileana, whose name seemed strange to me even if my father spoke it with immeasurable fondness. Both of them Jews, both worried at the start of a century which from its beginnings promised to be gruesome, both scared by the growing antisemitism threatening those close to them, at a given moment in the 1920s they emigrated together to Buenos Aires. There, in 1940, as news of the war that had broken out became grimmer and grimmer, and when the letters from the many relatives sent to the camps were already becoming scarce, there, in 1940, they conceived my father.

As for the other half of the family, the plot-line is less precise, perhaps because of my mother's narrative style, which is summary and diffuse, the evolution of worn-down stories that once bored her, perhaps because of the lack of a climax or a single central tension. Those origins took us back to an unknown region in Italy, but it was only later that I realised the name didn't actually support this, implying Spanish origins instead. From Spain, I believe, they set off for Peru with their aristocratic privileges, to make up a Catholic elite in Lima which some senile governor thought necessary. There followed generations of relative wealth, in material and anecdotal terms, highlights of which included the case of a great-great-grandmother or a great-great-great-grandmother who wasted away, starving herself out of love for a man, an episode my mother considered romantic. It must have been my grandmother Leonor, whom I remember only for her aura of solemnity when she was already living out her days in a wheelchair, who'd provided her with these potted biographies. She must also have summarised, in a tedious narrative, how she met Miguel, the Argentinian businessman who carried her off from the metropolis and took her with him to a hacienda in the pampas. My mother spent her childhood on that hacienda, in the almost exclusive company of her siblings, and, as she kept saying, constantly assailed by the dream that one day a plane would drop out of the sky to save her, and take her someplace interesting. She created her own salvation by moving to Buenos Aires, losing herself in the throng of every street corner, in the densely populated hallways of the university.

But I don't know why I'm going back over these trajectories, why I'm spreading myself so thinly among all these unnecessary details, which are as distant from our own lives as any novel. I think I always found it strange, whenever I heard these winding stories, when I learned about these faraway journeys, about this incessant displacement, about these many provisional dwellings, I think I always found it strange how attached my parents were to this city, this city they considered their own. If many of those who came before them seemed inveterate migrants, if many had made their homes mere outlines in the distant landscape, at the risk of forgetting their loved ones' old faces, their childhood hiding-places, why had they been so resistant to leaving the country that frightened them, and why should the pain they felt now be any different? I know it was an exile, a flight, an act forced upon them, but isn't all migration forced by some discomfort or other, some kind of flight, an incurable failure to adapt to the land you inhabited? Or might I, in these foolish musings, these inconvenient enquiries, be devaluing their struggles, belittling their paths, slandering the institution of exile that for years has demanded such seriousness from us?

11.

I see the young couple in a bleached-out image, a black and white photograph that time has faded more than it should have done. Something about their appearance makes them look strange, adding to the sense of anachronism – maybe the volume of their hair, the conspicuous pleats of a shirt, the solid stone bench where they sit, and something else I can't identify and yet which somehow immortalises them. Because they are my parents, and because they are not alone, because my father has a little girl on his lap, I know this is a record of the early 1980s, and yet it seems far more distant than that. These people I'm looking at are historical beings. Their singular appearance in the photograph is a culmination of former paths, one of many culminations of these complex lives that tangle around one another and are permeated by a collective past, by the march of an era, by cracks winding across time. I'm not sure how well I know them. I can't decipher their happy smiles. I don't fully understand the intricate arrangement of actions and chances that brought them together, but I know that I owe my existence, and the incautious words I'm writing here, to that union.

A child will never be the best person to appraise his parents' relationship, to understand what attracted one to the other, to unravel their feelings. He can't even wonder at the strange confluence that brought together a young Catholic girl of conservative origins and a Jew from a bohemian neighbourhood who was a follower of Marxism, because that would be to reduce them to watertight identities, to rigid types. Doubtless some drama was inevitable, but it would suffice to say that both graduated in medicine, that both attended the same psych residency, that they would soon both be psychoanalysts, for any mystery to be quickly dissolved. Another fiction, then, comes into being: they were not opposites at all, but two people alike, united in their criticism of the brutal and archaic psychiatric treatment perpetuated in hospitals across the world, and in their militating for a therapy that was more humane, more understanding, more comprehensive, less damaging. It's between one lie and the other that the drama of this narrative moves: no longer the petty dogmas of one family among many families, but the ideals of two young Argentinians at the tense apex of their political activity.

If those two young people were the same, certain mundane differences that invariably recur in common relationships didn't allow them to see it. I don't know many stories about them getting to know each other, about the period one might call courtship, but they all seem related to some idea of protection, to the conventional notion that it would be his role to protect her, providing the security which she, alone, would not find forthcoming from the world. A sudden braking on their way to the restaurant, his arm stretching out to hold her back, his hand flat on her thorax, precisely, an act of pure reflex and a heroic gesture she knew to thank him for – their hands laced together to celebrate the happy outcome. After dinner, the invitation for him to come up to her room, not because it was what she wanted, not because she had desires of which the old catechism would not approve, but because she was afraid, because she wanted somebody to check before her that there was nothing under the bed, none of the sinister creatures that in those days populated her nightmares.

They didn't go to his house as often, because he too was afraid. He feared the crash of shoulders against the door, he feared rough arms turning his things upside-down, he feared seeing himself lying face-down with his wrists locked into handcuffs, these were the dark pictures that troubled his sleep and brought him the chronic insomnia that I so often happened upon, my father as an unsettled shape lurking by the fridge. He also feared she would want to look under the bed, and find the guns he had agreed to hide.

I can see none of these fears in the photo, the photo is from another time. The smiles on their faces perhaps show the dissolving of their fear, its final relaxation, the at least partial truce they finally reached in some Brazilian square. My sister is not smiling, but she's only a baby – a smile from her would be no more than a reflex, some kind of spasm that nobody would think to understand. The only thing that's surprising is my brother's face. His lips stretch outward, tensing his cheeks, as if somebody were prompting him to smile against his will. His eyes are not light-coloured in this black and white photo, his eyes are scrunched up and almost impossible to make out, but I'm almost sure I can see some anxiety in his eyebrows, which sag under the weight.

12.

Guns under my father's bed. I think about those guns, I allow them to exist in my consciousness. From an extensive repertoire of false scenes I pick out an image of their presence: a few revolvers locked in a wooden box, a sheet covering the box with studied carelessness, all in the dim light filtering through the only open window, curtains trembling in the breeze. I don't understand the fascination they exert when I imagine them like this, in my father's house, under his single bed. My whole life I've had an aversion to these objects, an uncomfortable confluence of real danger and deadly symbol. All my life I've seen myself as a pacifist. Now I think about those guns and I don't understand the euphoria I feel, the vanity assailing me, as if the story of my father's life were conferred upon me: I am the proud son of a leftist guerrilla fighter and this partly justifies me, this redeems my own inertia, this inserts me precariously into a lineage of non-conformists.

I am the age my father was then — old enough to know that his guns are not mine, that it isn't up to me to grasp them and make him my brother in arms, that all that's left for me is to probe ideas, to try to understand those weapons. If I still have not understood, maybe it's because they were never a decisive bit of information, an uncontested piece of data, they have never existed without their own eloquent denial. No, we never had guns under our bed, my mother contradicts him with the same firmness each time, and each time he accepts, he conforms, he acquiesces. Then he allows himself to be carried away by a vague monologue about the utopian horizon of those days, the focalist theory of revolution preached by Che, the many Vietnams fought against imperialism, the Cuban Revolution as an auspicious example, the Sandinismo in which some of their friends also became involved. No, my mother gets annoyed now, Who?, she wants to know, and there follows a long list of names I've overheard in their conversations before, names that she listens to, waiting for the eventual slip: no, not him, Alberto, or Carlos, or Vicente, he wasn't mixed up in all that. What do you mean he wasn't, he even went to Cuba! He went to Cuba because his brother-in-law lived in Havana, my mother responds. He went to Cuba to do his training to fight in Nicaragua, my father insists this time, impatient now, having already forgotten the figure watching them in silence, the figure who doesn't know who to believe.

There's always a tension in the argument over these details, as if each little fact did not simply consist of itself, of its evident smallness, subjugated to some greater version of events. There are also relics of tensions left over from previous decades, a bygone reticence deferring every line they allow themselves to speak, an anachronistic sense of confidentiality, of unconfessable secrets, as if revealing this information and naming those involved were an indiscretion that would be censured by the movement – or, worse, punished by the tenacious executioners of a harsh regime. Sometimes they seem to lower their voices when they mention a specific incident, sometimes they stutter, they break stories off half-told, and I have the clear impression that they are still afraid of our ears

– that we are still, in their eyes, children to be spared the brutality of the world, or even dangerous double agents who will one day inadvertently turn them in.

But who, this is what I then ask, who would even be interested today in the petty meanderings of a distant time, and the answer my father always gives is an absurd mix of delirium and clarity: dictatorships can come back, you should know that. Dictatorships can come back, I know, and I also know that the arbitrariness, the oppressions, the suffering, exist in all kinds of ways, in all kinds of regimes, even when hordes of citizens march biennially to the ballot box – that's what I think when I hear him but I stop myself from saying it, to spare him the brutality of the world or out of some fear that he won't understand me.

Almost everything they tell me, they contradict; almost everything I want to tell them catches in my throat and discourages me. I know and I don't know that my father belonged to a movement, I know and don't know that he was trained in Cuba, I know and don't know that he never fired a well-aimed shot, that he just took care of people injured in street battles, looked for new recruits, preached Marxism in the shanty towns. He knows and doesn't know that I'm writing this book, and that this book is about my brother but also about them. When he finds out, he says he's going to send me the Operation Condor document in which his name appears. I ask him to send it, but I don't tell him I want to include it in the book, that I'm planning, ridiculously, to certify my invention with a document. Ashamed, perhaps, at his own vanity, he never sends me the file; I never ask him for it again, being ashamed too.

13.

My father never wanted me, he never wanted any of his children. I say this and I expect one reader to be moved, another to think they now understand something about me or about these alleged confessions, and a third who knows us to laugh at their folly. The fact my father never wanted children was something we learned with no surprise when we were already grown-up, with no melodrama, with some mocking laughter at his having lost the battle with destiny. Nothing about this resistance of his amazes me: if I myself, so compelled by those around me, by our implacable attachment to infinite propagation, if even I still resist carrying in my arms a child who is apparently mine, I can't help but consider my father's denial of fatherhood reasonable, this refusal at which he so conveniently failed. But my understanding comes through contrast, not resemblance. How could you want to engender a life if your own time is under threat from terror, if you doubt the very prospect of a new day, of any future, if every night you feel, foretold in shivers, the fragility of your body, the likely fleetingness of life?

What did always surprise me, however, was my mother's urgent conviction, her obstinacy about building a family, conception by conception, child by child. This journey, this self-denial, is something we've never been able to share a laugh about. I haven't enough details to describe the many obstacles they faced, the ever more intense day-to-day frustrations, the incessant search for some new method, for some unfathomable cause, for any reasonable response to their attempts – I haven't the details because she always left them out. Her drama was the drama of so many women and so many men, added to the turbulence the country was inflicting on her: like so many lives kept in suspended animation, the one she planned in her concave belly was deferred, and so her own seemed to be extinguished too, for months, for years, pregnant with impotence. No, that wasn't how it was, she might contradict me. Perhaps at that moment the desire to have a child was all she had left in life, another kind of struggle, a refusal to accept the annihilation being attempted by the regime. Having a child must always be an act of resistance. Perhaps affirming the continuity of life was no more than an ethical imperative to be followed, another way of opposing the brutality of the world.

But this opposition was not a success either, and with the sharp pain of failure, of multiple failures, with the substance of so many pains, a kind of mourning gradually set in. The imagined child on those unrestful nights, the child they spoke of in order to forget the routine fears and distresses, the child she touched in her belly in front of the mirror, this idealised child would not come, this child would not be conceived. I don't know how long it took them to admit defeat, our mother and our father, each in their own way. I know that together they decided to try adoption – or together they made the decision that, if she adopted, he would adopt too. She became pregnant with two promises on the same morning in 1976: the first doctor assured her that, if they persevered with the treatment, in six months it would work out;

the second offered to find a new-born to hand over to them before long. By this point they didn't mind, either of these paths would bring an end to their sorrow, either one would be welcome, would be the pinnacle of joy. Either one, whichever came first, the possible child.

14.

It takes four people, my father used to say, the plates already stripped bare of meat, silence settling over the house, and then a preamble that attributed the story to some inexact narrator from some distant time, then some more expendable comments deferring any suggestion of what it was going to be about, and then finally the motto: it takes four people to make a salad. A miserly one, an extravagant one, a wise one and a crazy one, as the amateur essayist who invented the parable had described them. It was the miser's job to dispense a meagre quantity of vinegar, the extravagant one's job to be profligate with the oil, it was up to the wise one to add just the right amount of salt, and then the crazy one would show up at the end and eagerly give the whole lot a good mix-up.

I guess we must have found it funny, my sister and I – we were children, we must have enjoyed those kinds of jokes, picking up lessons about existence and the evocative power of storytelling. But I remember once pointing out something that troubled me, making an argument I think valid to this day, and which to this day still comes back to me when I'm daydreaming, though it did and still does reveal my naïveté. Why couldn't the wise one deal with the whole thing, I asked. As a wise man he was surely able to take account of the different quantities, exaggerating when necessary, holding back

41

when necessary, and completing the preparation, at last, with all the strength in his arms.

My father laughed. I think my father laughed and there was a certain satisfaction in that laughter. It seems to me that on that occasion his derision was excusable, that his restrained laughter was a way of dismissing my excessive respect for wisdom and rationality. If he didn't contradict me, it was because he thought I'd soon learn for myself, that the days would take care of my omnipotence, force some humility into me. Each day does constrain me in this way, it's true, but I find it hard to learn. This was one lesson about existence I always struggled to take in.

15.

My memory of the troubles from some of the old days is vivid, almost palpable, carved with images that are too clear, too unmistakeable, for me to be able to mistrust them. Paradoxically, it seems harder to recount them if I'm obliged to uphold the concreteness of certain key facts, if all that's left for me to speculate about is their meaning. I won't allow myself to say that wasn't how it was – as my father once said, a foolish phrase, a clumsy phrase, the double negative obstructing his attempt at assertiveness. But here, I'll say it just once, I don't want to talk about my father. Here I want to talk about my brother, and the brother I was one crazy night, one clumsy night, and the brother who since that night I haven't known how to be, the brother I could never be again.

It was two or three years since we'd stopped sharing a bedroom, stopped sharing the silence and solitude, and each of us had exclusive use of his own silence and solitude, battling our respective ghosts in the small hours of the morning. But it wasn't my feeling of aloneness, or my fear of the dark, that made me seek nightly exile in his room – I was already older, nearly an adolescent, I would never have allowed myself something so fanciful. Perhaps it was out of habit, out of obedience to the inertia of those hours, but I like to think that in that place I also enjoyed the pleasure of being beside him, a pleasure that was vague, empty, and yet inalienable.

That night another solitude was added to ours; one of his friends was with us. Silence seemed inappropriate between us three boys, it needed to be filled with jokes and laughter, with jocular gestures that distracted us and at every moment affirmed who we were, what place we occupied in an intangible order. At one point, however, without understanding what had excluded me, I found I was no longer involved, I no longer had a place: they were two young guys chatting about something that eluded me, and I could only feel how very almost my adolescence was. If I'd been wise, I would have kept quiet, I would have held back. Not being wise, I used the ball in my hands as the words I was lacking and hurled it at the head of our friend, of my brother's friend. It wasn't rage, I am saying it wasn't rage and I think I'm right. Moments earlier he'd been covering his face with the palms of his hands, whatever he was confessing must have been serious or painful, and I thought he had his guard down, that it'd be funny to hit him. I could tell from the reaction that I was wrong, that I shouldn't have hit his head with the ball. That it wasn't a playful gesture but an unjustified act of aggression, an aggression unlike others, and which had no place among brothers or friends, no place in the camaraderie between young guys.

My brother threw me out of the room, but to say my brother threw me out of the room is imprecise – not just a distortion, but almost the opposite of reality. He didn't ask me to leave or kick me out into the hallway; he took me by the arm and led me in the opposite direction, into the room, to the door that opened onto the balcony. He sent me, just like that, into the night – a cold night, that's what memory with its dramatic inclinations is telling me – and he locked me out there, behind the glass door, the tall door that must have been twice my size, twice my age, that vast sheet of glass. With the cold and the rage

I was shivering now and I had no shortage of adjectives, my indignation was expressive and desperate, but it wasn't enough, it didn't mitigate the cold, it didn't pacify the rage. If I'd been wise I don't know what I would have done, but I wouldn't have kicked the door. I have no picture of that vast pane of glass shattering in one long second, that imposing sheet dissolving into a carpet of shards, nor can I imagine my brother's expression, scared or amazed at the unlikely spectacle, but I cannot forget the noise, the noise won't leave me, the infinite high-pitched collisions of glass against floor, the shrill song reverberating far beyond the word, echoing far beyond the act.

I ran, I must have run and shut myself in my room. I remember my eyes were dissolving into tears now and maybe that way I'd be rid of that picture, the picture of my brother on the other side of the glass breaking into shards. I wasn't afraid of the punishment he had predicted, I didn't think my mother was going to kill me. If I cried that much, a little boy's crying that hadn't assailed me in a long time, and if I punished myself there with voluntary seclusion, surely she would not enforce my punishment, she would certainly forgive me, seeing me penalised already.

I remember she came in and sat on my bed, next to me, and there was no rigidity in her manner. Perhaps she said the obvious − that I'd done something wrong, that I'd caused considerable damage, that we were lucky nobody'd been hurt, that she was disappointed − but I suspect she wasn't very emphatic, that she didn't claim the necessary authority, that she stayed a little longer, not to reprimand me or convince me of something, but to keep me company and assuage my feeling of helplessness. Here the memory is scarce: it seems unfair to say she asked me to respect my brother's space, his relationship with his friends, his privacy. It seems unfair to accuse her of such a contradiction, when so often, years later, she would beg me to seek him out, to break through his reclusiveness and invade the space in which he had shut himself away. No, it wasn't at her request that I shut myself away in my own space and in it created a set of habits, getting used to his absence, to his distance. It wasn't at her request that I no longer went back into his room like before, that I no longer went down the hallway with light footsteps, that I started knocking on that door with an imperceptible solemnity and asking, wordlessly, a little shy, if I could come in.

16.

They sat down at the table, at nine o'clock. Their hunger was great, the food was plentiful, but they found themselves compelled to postpone the suppressing of this void to the limit, to avoid sating themselves for as long as possible, because to satisfy their hunger would be to acknowledge their failure. No flavours would charm the palate now, no pleasure could be found in compulsory ingestion. Dishes still stacked up on the sideboard, cutlery in order, various roast meats pointlessly keeping warm, four arms hanging down the sides of their bodies, inert fingers pointing at the floor. It was supposed to be a dinner, the two of them were saying, regretfully. It was supposed to be an intimate, gregarious gathering, an opportunity for boasts and toasting, for involving themselves in laughter and trivialities, for fruitless drunken debates. It was supposed to be a dinner, not the mere satisfaction of a primitive need.

Nobody showed up, no guests, and nobody had said anything to them. With no hope now of a knock on the door, the two of them sat there not saying a word, their troubled eyes questioning the walls, questioning their own shoes. Why had everyone abandoned them? What had held them back or obstructed their coming? Could it have been a group abstention choreographed in advance? The dinner was for her co-workers, the co-workers at the hospital where she had just taken on a senior role, the co-workers she saw every day, with whom she shared coffees in the hallways, with whom she took the time to discuss serious cases, with whom she engaged in sober arguments about reforming that institution which had, at least inside its rooms, seen worse days. Round-the-clock co-workers, partners in the daily struggle, why had they disappeared, why had they fallen silent now?

Nobody would have said as much, and yet it was so obvious: they thought the place was dangerous. It's true that all gatherings were forbidden, all meetings of a subversive nature banned, but could a simple dinner be framed like that? Was this the extent to which life was proscribed, homes interrupted, friendships called off? Yes, because if that was what the others felt, all the people close to them, if they really did consider their home mined territory, how could they not have said anything, alerted them to the risk they were running? Staying silent in this situation, staying silent and abstaining, staying silent and disappearing, is staying silent in such a situation not betrayal? Without accusations, without a word, the two of them sat there, renouncing their hunger, abjuring their allies. Never had their vulnerability been so keenly felt, the windows so clear, the walls so fragile.

No record was kept of that night. Neither of them got up to fetch the camera, neither made any effort to memorialise it. For some reason, however, the scene reaches me as an almost static image, a millisecond snatched from the middle of infinity, my parents slumped at the table, their shoulders hunched, the steaming food still untouched. I know I'm overdramatising when I see them like that, I know I'm giving the occasion too much weight, a weight it never had in their stories. But I think I'm dramatising this weight because I can feel it, because in some sense I can understand it, or I think

I can understand it. I know the frustration of a failed dinner. I know, perhaps, the uneasiness you feel when you can't occupy your own space. I know, albeit indirectly, the feeling of a house that's been taken over.

What I do not know, what I cannot understand, is the pain of other dinners cancelled that same night, the pain of other deprivations, other self-denials, other insistent questionings. Other arms hanging down by the sides of bodies, their fingers more inert than my parents', pointing at a floor that was much closer. I can't conceive of a suppression of the self being exploited to the maximum, the systematic destruction of the void that is the self, its transformation into an object of torture. I cannot imagine, and this is why my words become more abstract, the unspeakable circumstances in which staying silent is not a betrayal, in which staying silent is a resistance, the most absolute evidence of commitment and friendship. Staying silent in order to save the other: stay silent and be destroyed. Perhaps they were distracted that night, my parents, but the question can't have escaped them. Those round-the-clock co-workers, partners in the daily struggle, why had they disappeared, why had they fallen silent now?

17.

In the world in which I live the streets have become inhospitable, and although occupying them is an imperative, the person occupying them is never actually at peace. In the world in which I live the streets have become the home of uncertainty, threat, danger, and anybody who wants to protect himself goes back home and shuts himself in his room, cloistering himself away in his own domain. In the world in which my parents lived, in that world, even these logics were twisted into incomprehensibility, squalor was twisted to make it more squalid still. Protecting yourself then meant keeping your distance, inhabiting the streets for as long as possible. In the world in which my parents lived, home had become inhospitable.

It was an October morning when my father found terror, or the traces of terror, in his consulting room. He only had to push the smashed-in door to be faced with a chaos of strewn papers, fallen objects, broken glass, the whole mundane everydayness transformed into an inorganic cemetery. The consulting room hadn't just been invaded and ransacked, it had been destroyed with military rigour, or comprehensively tortured so it would give up its accomplice. Of the few items my father saved without giving the matter much thought, one thing resisted, surviving through the decades and successive houses, the only memento of that desecrated space: a statuette of the Buddha with arms raised, which used always to hold his books, in a courageous role he was no longer able to fulfil. Having fallen to the floor, legs and arms broken, the statuette was now just a useless rock, but it kept its distinctive broad smile.

I don't know how much my father smiled in the months that followed, months in which fear drove him from his consulting room, months in which caution kept him away from home. His new routine was one of tireless displacement, avoiding the threat in borrowed consulting rooms, meeting other militants in bars, postponing his doubts in other family homes, in friends' apartments, in rented rooms. Sometimes he'd stay in a cheap hotel under an assumed name; living then meant acquiescing to the plundering of everything he held dear, of everything that was truly his. On those nights he would read and write to pass the time and sometimes he really did escape himself as he thought about things, about the regrettable state of things, about the urgent need to transform them. But when sleep finally managed to cloud over him, and his usual insomnia would grant him no more than a numbed torpor, living became all about despoliation and neutrality once again.

As the year was drawing to an end his son arrived, the boy who would be his son, who would be my brother, and this obliged him to ignore all the dangers and return home, regaining the intimacy of the old days, recovering the life he'd had broken into. Living with a child required an unshakeable presence, inside the front door, the child within reach, and solid arms to hold him. Living with a child also restored that private space for those close to them, and it was now open to whoever wanted to meet the boy, whoever wanted to wrap him up and feel the completeness restored to their own arms. And many people did want to, many knocked on their door, many could feel that the present was also made of its obverse, of the other opposite of sordidness, it was also made of unexpected appearances.

All the activity didn't go unnoticed, and some of the building's employees came over to check them out. One day when my father was going out with his baby son strapped on to him, the doorman sidled over with a mixture of vigilance and curiosity, looking suspiciously at his face, then examining the face of the boy who had appeared from nowhere after this elusive man's long absence. Between the blue eyes of one and the blue eyes of the other he must have noticed a real resemblance, because he remarked with the most obscene complicity, with an almost grotesque wink, The lady's a saint!

That night the Buddha's smile was positively restrained compared to my parents'. Together in the same bed, sharing the happy insomnia cradled in their son's crying, my parents for the first time broke into the laughter that they would thereafter devote to this anecdote, laughter that comforted the guts, granting the body long-forgotten vigour and the blessed relaxation of its still-intact limbs.

18.

I'm looking for that apartment, the apartment where my parents lived. I'm looking for that apartment even though I know I won't be able to go inside. I'm on the corner of Junín and Peña streets. 'Junín and Peña' was how my parents referred to the place, the name the apartment took on in their casual stories. On the corner there are two almost identical buildings, each boasting its average-looking façade, its old portico, the nearly grey walls where the dust has tried to establish itself. For a moment I fret, my feet shuffle aimlessly, nothing can be certain, my hands clench into fists, everything I know is imprecise, I don't know which building to ring at.

But I press the first intercom within reach of my stiffened fingers and all the anxiety dissipates. Indifference takes over now, a kind of paralysis in my chest: I no longer care whether this is the building, whether this is the truth I desire, whether it was here that my parents were persecuted and my brother spent his first days, the first months of this life I'm pursuing at a distance. And if I feel so indifferent, and if I don't completely understand this effort I'm making, why don't I gather up this nearly broken body of mine and just make a break for it? Why, instead, do I long for the mechanical voice that answers me without bothering to hide its boredom, the doorman's voice urging me to keep going, with its restraint, with its mechanical yes?

No, that's what I answer, all hesitation. No, I'm not looking for anybody right now, I just have a few questions, if you'd be so kind as to allow me, and immediately I regret my ambivalence, my inability to decide between obedience and a tone of enquiry. He walks slowly over to meet me, and in his face I can see the same weariness as in his voice and his legs, wrinkles that do not indicate long-past laughter, only many years of indolence. I'm looking for a couple who lived here many years ago, I say, contradicting myself, trying to describe that couple and realising how many concrete elements, how many specific attributes I'm lacking, how all I have at my disposal are abstractions and contingencies. I explain that they lived here with a baby, back in the 1970s, and that they had to leave in a hurry, I'm sure *señor* you'll understand why. I explain, so as to cover the silence he offers me in return, that I want to see the space they left in such haste, and in doing so perhaps find out who they were, understand them better, get closer to them.

He doesn't let me through and stands there rather incredulously, or that's when I notice that his expression isn't incredulity but incomprehension, combined with an adamant uninterest. *¿Pero usted no sabe sus nombres?* Do I really not know their names, he asks, and I almost laugh when I understand how far I am from a reasonable conversation, from making any sense at all, how badly I'm failing to express myself with any sort of clarity. Yes, I do know them, I answer with a sigh that reveals my dismay, they're my parents, the baby is my brother, and I know where they are, they didn't disappear. I just wanted to see the apartment where they lived because I'm writing a book about it, and at this point my voice takes on a certain grandeur, an unjustified pride which I try to conceal, a book about that child, my brother, about the pains and experiences of childhood, but also about persecution and resistance, about terror, torture and disappearances.

For the first time, I manage to get a reaction out of the doorman, for the first time his slow face twists into an expression that is unexpected, which I can only decipher when it is translated into a burst of scorn. *Ah, uno más* — another one of those 1970s books, he says, already moving, throwing open the door and inviting me into the entrance hall, waving his arm in a broad and solemn gesture, *Adelante, usted pase, haga lo que quiera.* But despite his invitation to come in I do not move, I remain frozen at that old door, those grey walls, and I no longer know what to say. The paralysis has spread from my chest, through my feet and hands all the way to my fingertips. This is the wholeness I'm able to attain; the paralysis is my entire body.

19.

The birth is something I cannot invent. Nothing is known about the birth. I find myself musing now, so many pages later, that I should have been faithful to the impulse to delete those poor imaginary scenes, I should have bowed to my hesitation and kept quiet about that unfathomable event. That's not how it was, it was not tellable, my brother's birth. The white room or the oppressive, cavernous space, the sound of boots against the floor or the hands so expert in inspection, that's enough now, *basta*, they're all just disposable fictions, nothing but distortions. Let her lower her arms, that woman who was reaching them out, so out of control, that woman and her ruin, grown quite unexpectedly from my barren mind. Ignore the boy, too, the boy and his helplessness, the boy and his salvation, that boy who also was not my brother. The birth is something I cannot invent, I'll say it again, there is no information about the birth.

My brother was born two days after his birth, he was born in a distant house on the outskirts of Buenos Aires, a house of scant furniture and peeling walls, a house of closed windows – I'm describing it by pre-supposition. This is the house to which my parents headed apprehensively, down unpeopled streets, almost lost, arguing about the way with fake hostility, dissipating their anxiety in wilful tension. The call had come the previous morning:

one of the three women they'd been dealing with, a midwife who acted as a go-between, now had a child available with no fixed destination, a boy whose hours could apparently be counted on the teensy little fingers of his hands – the midwife also sometimes oscillated between austereness and emotion. The other couple for whom the child had been intended couldn't be tracked down, and it was important to give him a home before Christmas. In the background, beyond the midwife's voice and the static noises of the phone call, a child could be heard crying, its shrillness cutting through the morning. The fact my mother remembers this detail has always touched me, as if that cry were their first conversation, a dialogue between tears and silence, as if it tore through the space and brought forward the moment when she would hold him tight to her breast.

As for the moment when she did hold him tight to her breast, I'd rather not invade their intimacy, I'd rather not guess whether all the tension of the journey fades into smiles, all the anxiety that had built up over time. For now I'll leave this woman and the new-born boy. If I leave them, I trust she will turn into his mother, and the woman who would become my mother, and maybe he will turn into her son, the boy who would be my brother. I'd also rather forget the man who approached a little shyly and, using only his hands, enclosed the smallness that was this boy, this fragile body under construction. He was not yet a father, subsumed as he was in the feelings of strangeness he discreetly hid, in the subtle numbing to which he would only admit some decades later.

I leave the family there, in a process of gradual composition.

20.

I leave the family there and move into the next room, I move into the next hour, I move into the deadlock that set in. Knowing the child's exact origins is never the best way, the midwife insisted, backed up by several books my parents knew by heart. There is a danger of placing a weight upon the family, an exaggerated attachment to the information. Names and circumstances can encourage excesses of speculation, uncomfortable feelings of empathy, the understandable vice of compassion. Giving a child up can be a painful act, a hard sacrifice, said the midwife, or expounded the books, but how many hard sacrifices do not keep their reasons intact? And in order that they might better understand what she was saying, and to yield a little to the couple's interest, she recounted the briefest of versions in an elliptical plot-line, the only version my parents would ever have about the child who appeared, the only one we would ever hear about my brother's origins.

He was born to a little Italian girl, said the midwife, not bothering too much about the vagueness of this description, the double ambiguity that such attentive listeners couldn't help but pick up on. Was Italian her nationality or her ancestral heritage? And as for that word little, so out of place, was it to suggest the youth of the pregnant woman or the slightness of her build? None of this was relevant, argued the midwife, or none of this were my parents able to decipher. He'd been born to an Italian girl who'd never wanted to get pregnant, and before long her partner had gone off, left unceremoniously and with no intention of taking any responsibility. Rejected by this lad, the girl now experienced a second rejection, by her Christian family who couldn't accept her. Which is why, on giving birth to the child, she had decided to give him to somebody else: her sacrifice came from a fear of solitude.

I don't know how my parents left that house, I don't know whether there was some weight slowing their steps, some primordial pity. I know that all I can do is return home with them in that car, travelling back next to my brother, and that I mustn't get lost in the streets of that distant neighbourhood, in search of the little Italian girl, of her solitude, of her pain. Was there pain inside that car too, as well as relief and joy, or only a silent doubt? My mother said nothing, for many years she would not speak of it, but the truth was that she was already scared of knowing too much, she was scared that the girl might appear at the next corner, at the next set of lights, fists hammering on the glass with incontestable passion. My father drove without pressing down too hard on the accelerator, reading each road sign as it appeared, go straight for the centre or back onto the ring road, so many possible routes, so many questions. Wasn't it worth looking into who the Italian girl was? And how much could they trust such a cursory account? How much would the boy want to know one day, when he could no longer fit inside his hands, and how much justice would there be in that yearning, how much right to ask?

I return with them in the car and I too am silent, I don't know how to answer these questions. I remain with them in the days that follow, in the apartment I never once entered, trying to watch the boy with their alert eyes, searching his face for some vague trace of the name that might represent him. This is an anxiety I share: so many days and they didn't give him a name, so many pages and I don't give him a name, either in this book where I know already that I shall not name him. I remain with them for so many years afterwards, although now, or still, there is space and time separating us. I am like them in a museum in Florence, finding or wanting to find my brother's face in a painting by Filippo Lippi, in any light-eyed angel some Italian girl might have conceived – though not knowing for sure, and perhaps never knowing, what the devil this angel confirms.

I am also standing beside my mother when, with exaggerated discretion, she puts a piece of paper away in a drawer. On this worn, aged paper, is a note, in her own handwriting, of the name and phone number of the midwife – the name in which, only much later, my parents would spot the evidence, the same name as my brother's when reduced to his regular nickname. Just like my mother, I don't dare to dial this ancient number, I won't make it as far as the automated message announcing the obvious error, the call's non-existent recipient. I remain aware that none of this has anything to do with me, or I think I remain aware of this, and yet, I cannot forget that there is a piece of paper in a drawer.

21.

There's a photo of my brother from his first few days, or months, from his earliest times. His mother, the woman who would be my mother, holding him up, firmly and very close to her chest, in total surrender, as I see it, to the solid and palpable assimilation of his existence, to the appreciation of that presence in the centre of the world that is that photo, in the centre of the diamond shape drawn by her shoulders and elbows. I think she's making an effort to get to know him, the way every mother tries to get to know her son whenever he's before her, whenever she's watching him, no matter how many days, months or years old he is. I wonder, even though I should not, if she might regret not having given him shelter inside her, those nine months she lost out on, not having felt his palpitations deep in her guts, his satiation and hunger, his wakefulness and sleep, the tensing and stretching of his limbs. This boy has already lived through an infinity of experiences she knows nothing of, sensory experiences at least, but is that not so for every mother, always apart from, excluded from what's taking place within that other being, that other body that is not her own?

I would not, of course, be able to decipher the thoughts or feelings of this woman, this other body that is not my own. I can only look at her and try to get to know her. I've lost so many years closed up in myself, busy with other chimeras. I can't see her eyes in the photo, her eyes are covered by her hair. It is with her smile, then, that she watches him, that she watches the centre of the diamond drawn by her shoulders and elbows, that she watches my brother, this being who is not me.

My brother, however, is not watching her. He is craning his neck to look behind him with considerable effort, his eyes avoiding her eyes and her smile. I, though, can see his eyes: they are surprisingly alert. I wonder what he is trying to look at, what he's searching for over his own shoulder, far from the diamond-shaped embrace in which his mother has him enclosed. This keen interest shown by my brother seems strange, a curiosity quite unlike him. I wonder, even though I should not, what vague relics might still inhabit his body or his mind, left over from those nine months in which he inhabited another body, a body absent from the photo I am looking at. In this moment, have the interest and the relics altogether dissolved? And if they have, if they no longer exist within him, what unsayable absence have they left in his fledgling body, what distance from that other body that used to be his, from that first house made of flesh and heat and fluidity?

These are futile questions, I know that, illogical questions required or suggested by the photograph. It's only because the photo stays silent that I am obliged to speak for it, that I insist on translating its rhetoric, on capturing its meandering judgement. And it's only when I stop looking at them, only when I close the album and stuff it onto as high a shelf as my fingers will reach, that I finally understand how photographs can lie with their silence.

22.

I learned from my parents that every symptom is a sign. That, very often, against reason, against the rigidity of the throat, the stillness of the tongue, the body cries out. That the body, when it cries out, comes much closer to the heart of things than reason does, because the body is more urgent, it sees no point in holding back, it wastes no time in lying. However, my learning this was something that happened rationally, and ever since that moment my failure to feel has been a sensitive matter, ever since that moment every cry of the body has just intrigued me.

I think about how my parents would have felt when my brother started rejecting the milk they offered him. That he wasn't going to be breast-feeding was obvious from the start, this was something his mother's body could not give him, in this regard his desires would not be met, the greediness of his lips, the tactile thirst of his tongue. In those first moments, holding him to her chest meant an unbreachable distance, skins separated by fabric, his mother's hands insinuating a plastic breast, the rubber in his mouth slightly cold, impossible to confuse with her body, an alien material intruding upon him. Still, for a few days he fed diligently, he undertook to grow as much as he was meant to, he eagerly fulfilled the purpose of his existence.

To say that he started rejecting the milk is imprecise. He would settle as before into that soft chest, his trembling lips showing his interest, scratching the plastic with his still incapable fingers, begging her eyes with his. He would suck up all the milk with undeniable force, and only then came the rejection, only then did an indistinct cause meet its effect: all the milk returned in a powerful jet, expelled like a foreign body from his own body, like a poison, the explosion of a tiny organism fighting for breath, like a rebirth. And the sequence would be repeated more desperately each time: the boy's hunger increased, as did his urgent longing for the milk, the distress of the person wanting to feed him, and a wounded desolation, perhaps.

At forty days old, my brother had an operation at last, and the cycle was broken. Pyloric stenosis, he was diagnosed with, a narrowing of the opening to the intestine that blocks the passage of food, causing a contraction of the stomach and violent vomiting. I now read the words the doctor would have said and imagine my parents' relief when faced with the clarity of this explanation, which was so convenient, with a piercing symptom that had so little meaning: a simple developmental problem helped along by genetic predisposition.

I imagine my father in the hospital, as he's described it so many times, leaning over my brother's crib, staring intently at his face, full of pity for his suffering. Such hunger in that little child's body, such hunger and yet he could not eat. Hunger in such a small body can only mean pain, a pain that adults avoid through their daily devotion to food, their respect for meals, their strict discipline. A few hours before the surgery they handed my father a tiny bottle, for him to feed to the baby if he could. There was such a paltry amount of milk that he almost rebelled against this treatment, he dreamed up conspiracies, they wanted to starve the boy to death, out of prejudice, for not accepting the family that they were. He restrained himself, however, and applied himself carefully to the task. When there was no milk left, when the boy's tiny nails had started scratching his fingers, when the blue eyes of one were entreating the blue eyes of the other, eyes so easily confused you could no longer tell whose were whose, he knew at last how close to him this being was, he knew at last that this son was his.

If one day my brother were left without a face, I would still be able to recognise him by the mark the surgery left on him, I would know at once that this brother was mine. So many times have I seen the scar on his belly, a scar much bigger than it needed to be, enhanced by the years that should have undone it, that should have diminished the memory of the cut to a fairly discreet mark. Is every scar a sign?, I wonder, involuntarily. Does every scar cry out, or is it just the memory of a cry, a cry silenced in time? I have seen it so many times, so easy to recognise, and yet I can't say what it is that it's crying out, that scar, or what it's keeping silent.

23.

Today I dreamed about my brother's death. I say today so as to fix it in time, to distance myself from it. I've just dreamed about my brother's death and I still feel the dream latent within me, which is why I hurry these words along, subsumed in unease.

Just a few steps separated me from the door to his bedroom, and on seeing the door open, simply seeing the door open, I concluded that he was not there. I didn't dare go in, but I didn't draw back, I shouted to my sister and she didn't appear, I shouted to my brother's friend, the one who had been in his room on that long-ago night, and he answered me only vaguely, he brushed me off with excuses. I stepped through the doorway and saw my brother's bed made, his quilt sagging like a shroud. The quilt sagging like a shroud might be something I'm making up now: it was in the made bed that his death was revealed.

In the fists I clenched tight, I could sense the scale of my rage – it was rage and not pain that drove my nails into my palms. Rage that for some reason I was unable to locate, rage at myself for not having realised, rage at my mother for not having told me, for having subjected me to the horror of this unexpected discovery, the horror of an absence no word could ever tame. I lay waiting on the bed for her arrival, on the bed that my brother had left empty, on the quilt that was his shroud. And soon there was neither pain nor rage, soon the rage had been transformed into sadness and I was crying, but when I touched my face I felt no dampness – neither rage nor pain nor sadness were things my sterile eyes could express.

The dream was interrupted by a selfish thought – by more than one selfish thought, it occurs to me now. In trying to invent his final hours, I wanted him not to have been aware of his imminent death, I wanted it to have been impossible to add up the regrets, to reach any simplistic final balance, since in this balance I would never be able to save myself. It had been almost a month since I'd spoken to him, since I'd said anything to him; it has been almost a month since I've spoken to him, since I've said anything to him. I wanted him, then, before his death, not to have had any chance to judge me, not to have known what a bad brother I was, not to have noticed how much I had abandoned him.

Later, still lying on his bed, it was the book that worried me. With his death, for some reason, the book would no longer make sense, I'd have to give it up, I'd have to tear all these hesitant pages to pieces, throw them in the limpid waters of some river, burn them in a hearth with a roaring fire – any hackneyed image would do. As if the book were a long letter to him, a letter he would never read (and if the book is a long letter to him, which is what I'm wondering about now, then I need to write it better, I need to make it more sincere, more sensitive). But the book is not a long letter to him, I thought straight after that, lying on the bed, I don't know whether awake or asleep. And then I went back to chanting, as if in a litany nobody was interested in hearing, that I need to tell his story, that his story, even if he has passed away, needs to exist.

I must already have been lying on my own bed, fists unclenched now, when that last feeling stunned me, that hybrid of freedom and duty: if his story needed to exist, and if I could tell it now with all the detail that previously I used to censor for him, then I needed to talk about his conflicted relationship with food, then I needed to describe how he abandoned his body, how he didn't feed himself, how scrawny he had been in his final days.

24.

He was not scrawny, those were not his final days. Something of that sorrowful tone, however, tended to mark our conversations whenever he didn't show up, when he shut himself away in his bedroom and refused all our entreaties, refused even the plate we offered him at his door, after which we'd stop confronting him and give up. He was too thin, that was what we believed or feared, the four of us confined to the table, covering up his absence with agonised words.

He was too thin and that thinness made no sense, it had no history, no discernible cause. Uselessly we questioned our memories, searching for pieces of evidence, for markers that defined this gradual, imperceptible process. When did his resistance to joining us at the table become a rejection of food? When did he stop wanting to keep himself strong, solid, dignified, feeding the energy that had always been part of him? At what point did he decide to give up on exercise, reduce his liking for sports to an indifference, limiting himself to the role of a passive spectator? On which distant morning did he wake up and decide to restrict his appetite once and for all, practising nothing but this restraint, exercising his body in controlled scarcity?

We were exaggerating, obviously, as I'm still exaggerating now, conscious that words distort, that questions can also assert. I don't want to, I cannot make my brother a hunger artist. I don't want to describe a pale face, or protruding ribs tearing at the scar, as if I were inventing some character for a new book, in the forge of one more astonishing or sad spectacle. I don't want to, I cannot exhibit him in a cage whose bars are these very lines, for the entertainment of an audience anxious to feel something, to nourish their compassion, to feed their altruism.

Maybe that's what we were doing while we ate, while we discussed my brother's difficult situation, as we defined it, not so much the thinness, but the inertia of this guy who had become inaccessible to us. We were suffering, that much is obvious, the distress visible on my parents' faces, a distress my sister had already learned to express and which was perhaps reflected in my own face, my teenage or adult face, a distress that I perhaps felt too. I suspect we weren't really looking for a way to reach him, to hug those slender shoulders, put a hand on his neck, andd tenderly, carefully, use our fingers to indicate the direction of the next step, to guide him out of the bedroom and into life. I fear all we did was observe the situation and think the obvious things, repeating the same preposterous questions. I suspect that we, cut off as he was in his bedroom, in front of the distracting screen, I fear that we were no more than passive spectators keenly watching their sports, watching another compassionate spectacle.

How to gain access to the difficult situation? How to elucidate its complexity if so many ideas were forbidden, if thoughts were broken off? One day I heard a university lecturer, digressing from the literature she was discussing, say how common it is for conflicted feelings about adoption to be expressed through an eating disorder – that very often, for the adopted child, eating means belonging, gaining weight means occupying your space in the house, occupying your position in the family, and in this way a simple longing is transformed into an exaggerated hunger. I thought about my brother, naturally I thought about my brother and what such a dramatic reversal of this behaviour might mean, but when I arrived home I refrained from mentioning it to my parents. There was no point surrendering to a conversation I could predict: together, word by word, we would reject the over-simplicity of the explanation, its automaticity, its generality. Together we would say over and over that an adopted child cannot be reduced to this primordial aspect, cannot be made into a schematic character. I'm not sure why I don't keep quiet on these pages what I kept quiet on that day. I think we would have been right at the time, I think I'm wrong now.

25.

But there are sorrows that are not susceptible to argument, there are pains not subject to exaggeration. There are stories that are not made up at the table, between gulps and forkfuls, between one chat and another, stories that steer clear of lightness, that do not lend themselves to common ruminations, to everyday words. There are events that do not live on the surface of memory and yet will not allow themselves to be forgotten, will not allow themselves to be repressed. All forgetting can fit inside a pain, that's according to a line of poetry about these uncertain things, but lines of poetry don't always get it right. Sometimes all that fits inside a pain is silence. Not a silence made from the absence of words: a silence that is absence itself.

I don't remember when I first heard the name Martha Brea. Most likely I didn't notice the weight invested in the name, I didn't immediately realise what it represented. For a while it must have been just some old name, for a friend of my mother's who used to come round to our house, who had grown distant from my mother for no reason. It was a passing comment from my sister, no doubt spoken in a more loaded tone, that led me to discover she wasn't a friend like any other, distanced by time, by exile, by the gradual spacing-out of letters received until no contact remained. I learned, without much detail, that there were no letters from this friend, that there never had been letters, that a label had been printed in red over her name: Martha Brea, disappeared.

She worked with my mother at the Lanús hospital, a hospital of which so many people were proud, an enclave of the country's anti-mental-asylum movement, an embodiment and symbol of this movement with which the two of them so enthusiastically engaged. One year earlier the director of psychiatry had been removed, by an order as obscure as it was unchallengeable, and my mother had been chosen to fill his position, while Martha would coordinate the adolescents' division. That year the two women's fondness for one another finally solidified into friendship. They travelled the long distance to Lanús together, came back together, exchanged confidences which in different times would have been tame but which now entangled them in a whole range of complicities. In the story of my brother's birth, her name appears: Martha was the first person to visit him at home.

The last time my mother heard her voice was at a meeting of the board of directors, while they were discussing some minor problems, and a few minutes later, when the meeting was interrupted by somebody calling her for a quick consult, came the unexpected shrillness of her screams down the corridors, piercing the walls, crashing against the ears and the memories of those who were sitting there waiting for her to come back. Running to the main entrance of the hospital, my mother was able to witness the roughness with which they pushed her into a car with no license plate, and the sudden and distinctive way the car drove off, which would play itself over and over before her eyes. Perhaps our mental stock of images is finite: with each disappearance, with each reported kidnapping, my mother sees, or thinks she sees, says she sees this same car tearing dramatically away, disappearing round the first corner, the trace of its tyres on the tarmac.

I don't know how many hours it was before my mother was sitting in the Brea family living room, a sumptuous, aristocratic-looking room, communicating her anguish to Martha's sister, begging her to take action, to do something, and hearing an answer she never could have expected: she got herself involved in things she shouldn't have, she messed with people she shouldn't, now let her suffer the punishment she deserves. I'm only sorry how sad my father is, the disappointment in such a well brought up daughter, the young woman added in her spontaneous, almost unconscious cynicism, and it was all my mother could do to silence her distress and preserve that extra hurt inside her, on loan, for her friend.

I don't know how many days it was before she was at the police station, appealing to the police chief who was an old friend of her brother-in-law's, a childhood friend of my uncle from Entre Ríos. He smiled, this man with self-contained gestures and a friendly face, he smiled and tried to calm her down; he would just need a moment to go check. When he came back, his face was transformed into an impassive frown and his voice was grave: what is your relationship with this woman named Martha? How close are you to her? Do you, if I may put it like this, move in the same circles? Alert to this transformation, my mother forced herself to swallow down her friendship, to claim no more than the professional connection, she was just there as a hospital director concerned about her colleague. In that case I would suggest, the man was now pushing her out of the door, that you forget her name and never ask about her again.

My mother did not forget her name. She never forgot her name, even if exile would soon increase the absence, even if, in a few months, crude borders would separate them. My mother did not accept her being gone, clinging to any vague piece of news that reached her, a woman who'd been in the same cell as Martha, who talked about her courage, her solidarity, a woman who existed and was alive and had answers. My mother didn't stop asking, but silence became more common than words and bit by bit the absence came to fill the place her friend had once occupied, stealing her name, distorting the traces left in her memory.

It was only when she received that letter, thirty-four years later, the letter which transformed Martha Brea into Martha María Brea, a victim of state terrorism under the civic-military dictatorship, a young psychologist whose recently identified remains confirmed her murder on 1 June 1977, sixty days after her kidnapping at the hospital, it was only when she received that letter that my mother was able to rummage deep in the calcified ruins of the event, touch them, move them about, and construct from the silence of those ruins and her distorted features the speech she gave in tribute to her friend. In the pages of this speech I came to know the missing parts of the story, but I came to know something else, too: the discreet mourning my mother had been engaged in for decades, the rarefied meaning this incomplete death had established in her reality. And I came to know something else, from the pages of this speech: the atrocity of a regime that kills and, besides killing, annihilates all those around their immediate victims, in ever-expanding circles of other victims unknown, of mournings prevented, of stories not told – the atrocity of a regime that kills even the death of those murdered.

I never knew Martha Brea, her absence does not live inside me. But her absence lived in our house, and her absence lives in infinite circles around other unknown houses – the absence of many Marthas, different in their unrecovered remains, in their distorted features, in their silent ruins. Different in all things: alike only in the grief that does not yield, in the chat that isn't improvised at the table, in the pain that never flares up. Martha Brea was the name of the holocaust in our house, another holocaust, one more holocaust among many, and one so familiar, so close.

26.

It's necessary to learn how to resist. Not going, not staying, but learning how to resist. I think about those lines of poetry my father could not have thought of, lines unwritten at the time, lines he was lacking. I think about my father at the last secret meeting he was to attend, quiet among the rowdy militants, abstracted from the hubbub of voices. Resist: how much of resisting is the fearless acceptance of misfortune, compromising with everyday destruction, tolerating the ruin of those close to you? Does resisting mean managing to stay on your feet when others are falling, and until what point, until your own legs give way? Does resisting mean struggling in spite of inevitable defeat, shouting despite the hoarseness of your voice, acting despite the hoarseness of your will? It's necessary to learn how to resist, but resisting will never mean surrendering to a fate that's already sealed, it will never mean bowing down before a future that's inevitable. How much of learning to resist isn't learning to question yourself?

Quiet among the hot-headed militants, abstracted from the hubbub of voices, my father was giving himself over to the politics that always exists in self-absorption. Within him there were no calls to literal battles, there was no space for fury and courage. Where are they now, those utopian horizons? Where are the ideological considerations? How many important arguments had been lost in the minute detailing of pains, in the counting-up of the fallen? Why hadn't anyone noticed that new tactics were no longer being discussed, as they progressed toward that badly-treated new society, why hadn't anyone noticed the whole thing was becoming a clinic of failure? How did they not realise that politics was being reduced, in those stormy encounters, to a mere cry of agony?

Not going, not staying, but learning how to resist, that was what his thoughts said, but his eyes betrayed him and flickered between his watch and the door. Hot-headed or abstracted, everybody feared the same threat: in the large circle they made up, under the diffuse light from the closed windows, only one chair remained vacant. Time passed, the minutes hurried by, and the person who had called the meeting did not show up to join them, did not show up to bestow even the smallest amount of calm on the day. To the beat of that second hand that my father was following so closely on his watch, fear completing the incomplete circle, every five minutes another face would grow haunted, within an hour the whole room had succumbed. Had he fallen, then, the one who had called them together? And if he had, if by now he had been handed over to the military, how long could they wait there, sitting around distractedly, ignorant of the ill fortune that awaited them? When should they put into action their long-deferred stampede?

Learn to resist, yes, my father might have thought, giving over as best he could to his politics of self-absorption. Now, however, another more urgent question arose: go or stay?

27.

You all need to go, that's what he said in a decisive voice, a voice whose fervour seemed to suggest intense alarm, a voice whose firmness sought to hide its fragility. The person saying this had the authority of someone in the know, someone who has seen the ugly side of a world stripped of its masks, who has felt the hardness of the world stick into his soft flesh. The person saying this was Valentín Baremblitt, the psychiatrist from whom my mother had taken over the running of the hospital, arrested a year later for no legitimate reason, who had totally vanished more than a month ago and been out of contact right up until that moment when he called them together. He was thin and pale, this man who looked at them now with such seriousness, his hands trembling, his lips discoloured. You all need to go, you'll be next, those were his exact words, the tension cutting the false lull of the early morning like a knife.

And so, in this unforeseeable moment, in the fervour of a voice that somebody had failed to silence, in two simple, summary phrases, came the culmination of all the doubts that had assailed them for months, and any indecisions, any cryptic questions were settled. Staying was no longer an option, staying because the city belonged to them and not to the executioners, because in those streets life was happening and in those squares it was being turned into history, none of that sounded sensible now. Leaving was what they ought to do, not even stopping at home first. Leaving, just the two of them and the boy, just the three of them and what they had in their pockets, the clothes on their backs, a rucksack with a full bottle for the baby and a handful of diapers. Leave and forget about the defeat, leave and dodge the calamity, and keep what they still had, whether it was a lot or a little, the daily existence that was being stolen from them every day. Leave and also save that other life which had only barely begun, protect the boy wrapped in their arms, save their son, that was what my mother thought as they crossed the city in absolute silence, punctuated only by the regular rhythm of their shoes on the pavement.

The following morning they were already in my uncle's car, trusting in his extensive network of contacts, two aeroplane tickets bought just as an alibi, to throw anyone who wanted to ambush them off the scent, and in the trunk two suitcases full of whatever my aunt had gathered up from the empty apartment. I don't know much about this trip, there's something about it that eludes me, I have no idea what they talked about – I don't know if their departure was melancholy, or desperate, or if it already foretold a moment of greater calm, the welcome that Brazil would give them, these people who were not even planning to stay. I imagine the car crossing the sun-drenched plain and it's as though my gaze is pulling away, as if I'm seeing it from above, a landscape with a car speeding through it. This sharpens my awareness that I was not there, that I could not have been there, that this hurried crossing is an ancestral event from my own history, essential for some reason that I cannot properly explain, or which is not relevant.

I know they crossed the Uruguayan border without much trouble, that they said their goodbyes with quick, casual-looking hugs, that within hours the three of them were on a plane that would take them from Montevideo to São Paulo. One final shock came from the pilot's robotic voice, announcing to the passengers that there was a slight change of plan and they'd have to make a stopover in Buenos Aires, which in my father's imagination reawakened some old and feared images, rough searches, handcuffs, questionings. When, after some agitation, he discarded this possibility, what my father felt was something like relief, as if he could breathe again at last. There he understood, or began to understand, that not everything could be reduced to the few neighbourhoods where he had once lived, in the grip of terror and alarm. There he began to understand that the world was much vaster, made of broad plains and infinite horizons, physical or utopian, and that it would always, everywhere, make sense to preserve them. There he concluded, or wanted to conclude, that this defeat was circumstantial, a provisional defeat and nothing more.

It would be flippant to say that my parents did not suffer in their exile, that they didn't have to put up with its arbitrariness, its misunderstandings, its nostalgias, its unwished-for forgettings. I do, however, feel that to some extent they always experienced it as they did on that morning or that afternoon, as a peaceful landscape, a sun-drenched plain, a well-deserved calm after a stormy night. I don't think it would be an exaggeration to say that the years that followed were an extension of that day, at once tense and calm – even though we sometimes also revisited the night before, and even though I'm trying so hard, who on earth knows why, to recover it.

There's another night I can't forget, in a city far away from that world which had become so huge, closer to this one where I'm now starting to describe it. I was in Barcelona with my parents, we were having dinner with

Valentín Baremblitt, glasses clinking together in a happy choreography of drinks. In between Valentín's smiles, in between the stories he told, a shadow crossed his face, clouding it over for a moment, he stepped away from the table and lifted the hem of his trousers. His right ankle was swollen, red, deformed. You see my ankle? he asked my mother. They did this while they were asking about you.

28.

One day everything is alien. You walk down an un-known street and it turns an unexpected bend, although there is no corner it becomes another street, assumes a different name, and you are lost in what's supposedly your neighbourhood. One day everything is alien. Eventually you find a café, not because you want a coffee but so you can sit there for a while; the waiter brings you a cup and seems eager for you to leave, because in this place 'having a coffee' has a literal meaning that doesn't include lingering there for hours. At first we all found it a bit strange, my parents say, and I understand them inside-out, because I've already found the too-straight streets and the afternoon-long coffees strange myself.

One day everything is provisional. He is only in Brazil until they leave for Mexico, to resume the battle there alongside other exiled comrades. She is only in Brazil until they leave for Spain, to resume their lives there and the many plans that have already been delayed. It's because they don't make up their minds that they keep on staying, the months stretching out like winding roads, and in time the taste of the coffee actually becomes pleasant. One day you give some information to a passer-by and realise you know the name of the street you're on, that this might be your neighbourhood after all, that what was alien has become your own, or almost. You don't even care that the man doesn't understand your accent, you gesticulate and the still–lost man returns a friendly smile – there are griefs here, of course, there's a dictatorship here just like there, wretched poverty on every corner, and yet wherever you look people are smiling.

You smile and think you understand, although you do not understand, something about those people, something in them that's real about their happiness, about their beauty, about that alien beauty which one day you'll be able to imitate – when you'll manage, who knows, a similar lightness. You smile and wonder if perhaps beauty won't always be alien, if happiness won't always be alien, something nobody can recognise in themselves, something vanishing that you only ever see printed on other people's faces, never on your own. You ask yourself, that day, not if you'll ever be able to make beauty your own, make happiness your own, but if you'll ever be able to make yourself someone else, make yourself alien too.

29.

But a day came when the Brazilians didn't know how to smile either, a day when they covered their faces with spread hands, a day when the usual friendliness gave way to a more conspicuous anger. Hard to find the appropriate tone for the situation, to understand the importance of the unimportant, to respect the legitimate suffering that there can be in trivialities, especially when collective or shared. Hard to appreciate the full weight an insignificant thing can assume when various interpretations are projected onto it, when so many meanings crystallise within it. To move from the most banal circumstances to a feeling of tragedy, sometimes all it takes is a subtle slip, a minor error.

On that day there were six minor errors. A midfielder losing to a neat dribble, a good header left unmarked, an easy one-two inside the area, a defender who should have jumped, the apathy of the goalkeeper, and once again the apathy of the goalkeeper, his visible lack of interest in reaching the ball, in fending off any attack. In an incredible rout by Argentina over Peru, six-zero, it was Brazil who got knocked out, albeit unbeaten, albeit undeserving of such bad luck. Or was it not bad luck? With everyone gathered together in the same house, exiled Argentinians and Brazilians in solidarity, everybody was now exchanging suspicious glances, barely able to hide their aggression, their speech sharp now, the words they exchanged coarse. All of a sudden, the eleven men on the field were worthy representatives of a country lacking in character, an unworthy country, that whole game was a con, a dirty trick, someone had bought the goalie, and each of those Argentinians present was strangely implicated, they had their share of responsibility, each of them had contributed something and was complicit somehow.

Complicit with a characterless country that was persecuting them, that's what they had become. However truthful they might have been, their protestations seemed ineffective. They had, it's true, refused to wear the shirt, they had restrained all their shouts, they had committedly booed every authority who appeared on the screen, every gleaming uniform that appeared before the cameras. Since the start of the Cup they had spoken up against the deception, railing against FIFA for sponsoring this nonsense in the first place, for giving the regime a chance to boast of its victories to the world, with its fake chants of freedom, celebrating its constructions, whether prisons or stadia. Yes, they had devoted themselves to all this abundance of criticism, and they still did, gesticulating in emphatic self-defence, but did they truly believe what they were saying? Were those actions enough? Weren't they contributing something, as they were accused of doing, weren't they complicit, just by absenting themselves, by having found a new neighbourhood, enjoying the taste of the coffee, and getting together, happy and carefree, to watch a football game? They were barely speaking now, as crestfallen as the others, suffering the defeat just as they were, an imitation of another defeat, and feeling more than ever the guilt that assails those who have managed to get to safety.

I don't know for sure, perhaps these are falsified musings, I can't help noticing the increasingly pitiful tone, the tone that overtakes me when I reconstruct these episodes. What remains of the story of that night is the laughable anecdote, tragedy once again transformed into farce. My brother crossing the wreckage of the living room and kicking a ball with all the strength in his scrawny legs, yelling enthusiastically in his Argentinian accent, *gol de Kempes!*, planting an insoluble seed of doubt over who it was who'd taught him that patriotic cheer.

30.

There is something I don't want to ask them. There are many things I don't want to ask again, which I'd rather conjure up from words kept in the darkness of my memory, words I've already forgotten but which my mind was careful to transform into vague notions, blurred images, uncertain impressions. From this immaterial debris I have tried to construct the edifice of this story, on deeply buried foundations that are highly unstable. There is something I don't know about, however, around the limits of this precariousness, something they never told me, and which I still don't want to, or cannot, ask them.

I imagine my parents, on that morning I don't know about, in an apartment I've never been inside, in a building of which I can only glimpse the façade, I imagine my parents at the table leaning over a newspaper. It wasn't common for papers to carry Argentinian news; it wasn't at all common for them to circumvent any official propaganda and talk about serious crimes, crimes against humanity, men and women kidnapped en masse, tortured, disappeared – the whole liturgy of repression reduced to a summary listing. It's a Sunday morning I'm imagining, in August 1978. Almost all the crimes were known about in those days, but news of them often arrived by the most tortuous routes: the rumours multiplying each time exiles met, and all those brutal personal experiences, many of them still unheard. It was strange to see this printed in the newspaper, albeit clandestinely, in a faraway country, in a language they hadn't mastered. An ambiguous feeling overtook them: the terror was finally being reported there, an attempt was being made to do justice to the severity of it, but this was also confirmation of the incessant rumours, what had been intangible in their own experience becoming tangible news.

At the foot of the page, in that newspaper I did not read, a brief notice in tiny letters was almost overlooked. It was signed by the Mothers of the Plaza de Mayo, or rather, by a faction of the Mothers of whom at that point nobody had yet heard, the group that called themselves 'Argentinian Grandmothers of Disappeared Grandchildren':

We appeal to the consciences and the hearts of those people who have in their charge or who have adopted or know the whereabouts of our little disappeared grandchildren, so that, in a gesture of profound humanity and Christian charity, these babies might be restored to the hearts of the families who have been living in desperation without knowing where they have ended up. They are the children of our children who were disappeared or killed in these past years. We, the Mothers-Grandmothers, are today making public our daily cry, remembering that God's Law protects the most innocent and pure beings of all Creation. The law of men also grants these helpless creatures the most basic right: the right to life, with the love of their grandmothers who search for them every day, tirelessly, and will continue to search for them as long they have breath in their bodies. May the Lord shine his light upon those people who receive the smiles and caresses of our little grandchildren, so that they might respond to this anguished appeal to their consciences.

Would they have read this heartfelt appeal out loud? Would they have noticed a heat flooding their faces, leaving fleeting traces of a shiver up their spines? Would they have been struck dumb, wordlessly recalling that now distant series of events, the call just before Christmas, the house with the closed windows, the Italian girl? Would they have tried to persuade each other how unlikely it was, that there had been no suggestion, that soldiers wouldn't have kidnapped a baby only to hand it over to a couple they considered subversives? Would they have consulted a law book, to be sure that, although they were outlaws themselves, they could still have the law on their side, guaranteeing that 'the adoptee ceases to belong to his original family and all familial bonds with all its members are extinguished, such that nobody might at any time consider that child their own or bring a legal case about his parentage, his upbringing or his inheritance'? Would they, all the same, have opened that drawer I have never opened, just for a moment, seen the sheet of paper not yet quite so worn out, contemplated calling the woman who had given them a child, the child who was theirs, the boy who was so full of life and so beloved, who was now asleep in the next room?

No, these are not the right questions – and perhaps that is why I have never asked them. Speculating about how my parents might have reacted, about how they might have read the appeal from the Grandmothers of the Plaza de Mayo, is a fragile attempt to consign this appeal to a specific time, to remove it from time, to exclude it from the present in which its voice still exists. Since 1978 the appeal from the Grandmothers has been repeated: it's in the square where the women walk in silence every Thursday, it's in the papers I've been able to read many times, reproduced in several news articles. I don't know why I insist on turning to my parents, imagining how they might read it each time. Perhaps I lack the courage to understand how I read it myself, or how my brother would read it.

31.

I visit the Museum of Memory, I walk down the ominous corridors, I allow myself to be consumed once again by the same tragic destinies, the same sad journeys. There is a room devoted to the Grandmothers' cause, that's what the map tells me, and I follow the map with firm steps but hesitate once again when I reach the doorway. One sole couple are walking around the room, hand in hand, a slow circuit that doesn't seem close to ending. When I see them, from my place on the threshold, I realise I don't want to share that space with them, I don't want to submit myself to the delicate back and forth that those few square metres demand. Still standing on the threshold, visible out of the corner of their eyes, I feel my blood reddening my face, I feel a sudden shame I cannot decipher. I don't move, for seconds or minutes I don't move, but it's not long before the couple ask me to let them past and I take two steps forward – I put myself, perhaps against my will, in the middle of the Grandmothers' room.

There is nothing, there is almost nothing, the room is made up of nothing but rows of old photographs, images of disappeared women, the standard black and white pictures of the victims of the military dictatorship. They're smiling, these young women: a sensitive effort has been made to catch them in a moment of joy, to capture some glimpse of happiness, even if within a few months, or in some cases weeks, they would themselves be captured, violently, subjected to the usual torture despite being pregnant, fed only as much as was necessary for them to keep carrying the child, forced to give birth in horrendous conditions. There has been a sensitive attempt to give them strength and dignity: they are the daughters of women with strength and dignity, women who are now searching for the many kidnapped babies, appropriated by the military, handed over to families who were friends of the regime, passed from hand to hand like valuable merchandise, missing without trace.

Only one young woman pictured is not smiling. Her pale, fine lips seem to foretell the evil that is about to descend upon her, the evil that will descend upon all of them. Her light-coloured eyes have a sadness to them that spreads beyond the photo, that restores to the room the mood that somebody wanted to avoid. When I see her, I notice an involuntary impulse in myself to scrutinise her face, to examine each of her features carefully. When her appearance turns out not to be familiar, when it no longer reveals anything to me, I move on to scrutinising the other faces with exaggerated interest, guessing at the colours of their eyes, tracing the curl in their hair, the delicate line of their noses, the curve of their jawbones. Why I do this I don't know, or I don't want to know, I cannot confess it, even to myself.

On my way out of the room, by the door, there is a wooden box with a narrow slit, which looks like a suggestion box. *Make your contribution of information herein to assist us in locating the grandchildren still missing*, says the note stuck to the box, in that formal imperative voice so distinctive to Spanish. For a moment my feet betray me, I'm an indecisive shape on the threshold, I don't know if I'm coming in or going out. I can't disguise the distress

I'm feeling: I wonder, though I cannot, whether I have anything to contribute, if I can help the Grandmothers in their struggle.

32.

I know that I am writing my failure. I don't really know what I'm writing. I waver between an incomprehensible attachment to reality – or to the paltry spoils of the world we usually call reality – and an inexorable pull towards telling tales, an alternative gimmick, a desire to forge the meanings life refuses to give us. But even with this double artifice I can't attain what I thought I desired. I wanted to talk about my brother, about the brother who emerged from out of my words even if he was not the real brother, and yet I resist this proposal on every page, I flee whenever possible to the story of my parents. I wanted to deal with the present, with this noticeable loss of contact, with this distance that has arisen between us, and instead I stretch myself out along the meanderings of the past, of a possible past in which I distance myself, and lose myself, more and more.

I know that I am writing my failure. I wanted to write a book that discussed adoption, a book with one central question, a pressing question, ignored by so many, neglected even by leading writers, but what would there be to say in the end? What uncertain truth could I tell about those lives I know nothing of, marked by a tiny initial abandonment, or maybe not even abandonment, maybe merely personal circumstance, accidental as any other, arbitrary as any other, resembling how many others? What would I have to offer apart from fears, observations, questions? I wanted to take my brother as an example and turn him, somehow, into something greater: assemble a case in which somebody would recognise himself, in which some people would recognise themselves, and which spoke like a pair of eyes. But how could my brother possibly represent anyone else, if in this book he doesn't even represent himself? It's an unfair role I've cast him in, my brother as a hostage to what he will never be.

I know that I am writing my failure. I don't really know who I'm writing to. I think about the piece of paper hidden in the drawer, I think about the phone call nobody made, about the obvious error this call would lead to, finding nobody on the other end of the line. Quite without subtlety, I find myself afraid: maybe this book is the error, created for a non-existent addressee. I return to the origins of my impulse: I wanted, I think, the book to be for him, for its pages to speak what I've so often kept unspoken, for it to redeem so many of our silences. It isn't going to be like that, it wasn't like that, I see that now. This book won't empower me to get him out of his bedroom — and how could it, if in order to write it, even I have had to shut myself away? Now I no longer know which way to go. Now I am paralysed in front of the letters of the alphabet and I don't know which to choose. Now, yes, for just a moment, I can feel it: I want to have my brother here, resting his hand on the back of my neck, pressing with alternating fingers, so gentle, so subtle, to guide me where to go.

33.

Once a year, however, my brother would go against his usual restraint, he would withdraw from his withdrawal, retreat from his retreating, turning long drawn-out scarcity into the potential for excess. He would burst from his bedroom with an energy none of us could ever have imagined, even though the same thing happened every time, and set about making his way through the house, moving furniture, clearing spaces, eliminating any obstacles that he might find blocking his path. He would also burst out of the house, passing through various neighbourhoods in his wanderings, acquiring festive props, musical instruments, big loudspeakers, meeting old friends and making new friends, and new friends of friends, summoning everybody to his event with the greatest effusiveness. The kitchen, where most of the time we hardly saw him, then became his fortress, where he would hide behind great barricades built from boxes of meat and drink, an immeasurable quantity of boxes that he never seemed to tire of ordering.

There was some pleasure seeing him, on these birthdays of his, transforming all his accumulated passivity into action, stepping beyond his reclusiveness and becoming sociable – a pleasure to watch all that was mean in him transformed into prodigality. A pleasure that closely resembled relief, it's true, the sight of this unexpected joy in him, and if not joy then something very like it, a euphoria we made considerable effort to keep up with. For two or three hours we would all be there, animated by his animation, laughing at his laughter, until we reached an unspecified limit that we were unable to pass. Anybody watching his incessant coming and going in the following hours would be very impressed at the quantity of drink and meat that skinny body could manage. Bit by bit, well before this, our pleasure became a fear, then a certain distress which, though we didn't acknowledge it, was the secret motivation for each of our departures. Discreetly, in the middle of the party that gave no indication of its ending, as the euphoria noticeably dissipated, my parents would withdraw to their bedroom, my sister would wander over to give him a kiss and then go out, and I'd invent some reason to leave the house, and in this way we would vacate the space he had made an effort to fill.

How long each party lasted I couldn't say; I know how long the one I returned to lasted. That night, while I was busy keeping myself distracted, I missed a series of calls translated into messages that conveyed a great anxiety, almost a despair I couldn't understand. The party was going on too long, that's what they said, the party was overflowing with music and commotion and chaos, my brother's drinking was out of control, my sister had an important exam early in the morning, she wanted to study and couldn't, she wanted to rest and couldn't, my father had said something thoughtless to my brother, and then my brother, according to my father, had exploded. When I arrived, the situation was already beyond any explanation those messages could offer; everything was nearly normal, the party was carrying on with its potent beat, but my sister's eyes, and my father's, and my mother's, spoke of a sadness their words could not.

I never really found out what happened that day. I heard their words like a person being told an implausible plotline, though I was sure they weren't lying. I understood that what they expected of me was something far beyond my capabilities, a kind of mediation that seemed impossible. I went to find my brother in the crowd, and by the time I spotted him he was already heading towards me. In the middle of the living room the two of us stopped, his eyes red and blue, his eyes choleric and crystalline. I don't know if what I understood at that moment was what I deduced from his eyes or what his words were saying. I'm not like the rest of you, I think I heard, and I think the tone of his voice was angry and sad. I wasn't born to spend my whole life thinking and reading and studying. If they're disappointed in me, fine, I know it's not what they want, I know I'm not the model son, but can't I just enjoy my party today? Isn't this my house too, can't I live here in my own way, with the music I want? It's OK for there to be noise here too, there can be a racket here too, it's not a library, this place. Fuck, I screwed up, I know I screwed up, but he screwed up too, I screwed up because he screwed up, because she did too, and her, because everybody's screwed up.

No, this is a fiction, and not even a very convincing one. I don't really remember, I wouldn't be able to remember what my brother said, I can't attribute a speech to him that is too precise, or too vague, a speech that has been lost in its excess or its scarcity of meaning. I remember that we stood there a moment, in a conversation that was muffled by the intensity of the noise, a dialogue between desolation and compassion, between understanding and a cry of anguish. I remember that this time I knew to acknowledge he was right, tentatively I said something that seemed to soothe him, and as he was soothed so was I, though it was ephemeral and unexpected. I couldn't say which of us leaned his body in first, which one of us propped up the other, who then wrapped his stiff arms around the first – I can't say what didn't matter to us. What matters is that we hugged as we hadn't for a long time, and we cried as we hadn't for a long time, as I don't remember us ever having done before.

Then I felt a friend of his pulling at his elbow, kidding that that would do for now, that there was another beer waiting for us. This time I stayed for the whole party, and I was able to watch his friends head off one by one, so late now, distracted, always leaving him with a quick squeeze of the shoulders, affectionate and genuine.

34.

I had another brother, though it would be more precise
to say I didn't have another brother – that only my
brother had another brother, and maybe not even he did.
I had another brother I never met, whom nobody met,
whom only my mother was able to feel in the intimacy
of her body, whom only she could hold in her belly, a
brother who died shortly before he was born.

The pain of that story always eluded me, and I don't
think I've ever been sensitive enough to take it in or
understand it. It's the pain of a story I am reluctant
to tell, as though I were invading territory that had
nothing to do with me, as though I were going against
my mother's wishes without knowing why. There's one
thing I don't want included in the book, she once said to
me, don't say I only managed to get pregnant in Brazil.
She didn't want anybody to think, or this was how I
understood her reticence, that her previous inability
lacked concrete causes, that it was merely a psychological
response to the situation in which they were living. She
didn't want anyone to consider, this was what I deduced
without saying anything, that there was blame in her not
conceiving a child and that the blame was hers. But even
if her reasons were simple, even if they were unambiguous
in a way that reasons never really are, what cause could
be more concrete than that insistent uncertainty, life as

a taut thread ready to snap? What other element could redeem her from that blame, that non-existent blame, more than this?

For years my mother struggled to get pregnant, she went to various doctors, subjected herself to treatments that boasted of being the most modern – when it comes to this process, I'll say again, the well-worn, generic description is all I have. Arriving in Brazil, now with a child whose crying cut through the long silence in the next room, now with a child whose body occupied the empty space opened up by the old longings, arriving in Brazil, although it didn't need to be like this, the promise of so many doctors was finally fulfilled. I imagine this woman standing at the mirror, hands resting on the bulge that outlined a new womb around her navel, feeling this living thing forming slowly beneath her fingers. I imagine this woman with the passing of the months, eagerly watching the gradual expansion of her silhouette, getting used to the baby's movements, now subtle, now, violent, feeling a new focus for the world concentrating inside her, discovering the strange fullness of being two people under one skin.

I imagine my mother nine months pregnant, worried at the unusual stillness of her soon-to-be-born child, rushing back from the beach to the hospital, telling herself and my father, not quite believing it, that everything was going to be fine. I cannot, however, imagine her receiving the news of the death of the foetus, the death of the child who already had a name, already had a bed, who would soon have a place at the table, I cannot or I do not want to imagine her suffering. For a week she still had to carry the lifeless child in her belly, in a lingering farewell to everything that was or could be, to the baby or the intended baby, to her son or his chimera. A lingering farewell culminating in the saddest birth you

112

can imagine, the birth of a dead child, or of the now dead desire to give birth to a child.

She is the one who speaks, and I hear her speak, about her despondency. She is the one who said she locked herself in the house and didn't want to go out again, ignoring her husband's entreaties, surrendering herself for a brief instant to despair. But there was a boy now, shy in a way he usually was not, a boy who demanded to be cared for, wordlessly begging her to take him in her arms, at this moment, right now. And in that moment, in that now, when she took him in her arms, he was the one who protected her, he was the one whose caresses silenced the implacable helplessness that had tormented her since the loss. There was a tortuous justice in that hard event: she'd carried a pregnancy to term, she'd given birth to a boy, and now she was holding a boy in her arms, skin against skin, her son, in a strange fullness that nobody could break.

I've never missed this brother I didn't have – on the contrary, his impossible existence usually inspires me to unsuitable questions. How many children did you want?, I ask my mother, and she answers without any hesitation that she always wanted three, perhaps to declare herself fulfilled and assure each of us of a specific place in her plan. I don't ask what would have become of me, the third, if that other child had survived – I control my narcissism, not wanting to sound so infantile. But I sometimes think that if that brother existed, this book would not exist, or maybe he would be writing it.

35.

In the photo album, there is a photo of my mother arranging the photo album. A curious record of memory being assembled, of a remote existence being transformed into narrative through an artful sequence of images; a curious notion of there having been something memorable about the very formation of memory. My brother, aged three or four, is leaning over the album with particular interest, or is leaning over my mother's hands as she arranges the album. Perhaps he's starting to take on that strange habit of recognising himself in other people's faces, whether that other is his father, his mother or himself. Perhaps he's starting to learn the strange practice of sensing himself in a variety of identities and describing himself – a practice he will try so hard to avoid years later. Seeing them, I think only the obvious: that this tale of mine has been moulded over time by my parents, that I cannot easily extricate myself from their version of the facts. Seeing them, I feel I am partly a being they've created in order to tell their story, that my memory is made of their memory, and my story will always have to contain theirs.

I turn the page and see my father lying on a bed with crumpled sheets, an open book with the cover folded back to allow him to hold it in one hand while the other brings a cigarette to his mouth. At the moment of the photo he is not reading the book: his face is turned to look at my brother, aged three or four, lying there beside him. With his little hand, the boy is trying to move the book up to his eye level. Between his fine lips, a pencil plays the part of an extra-long cigarette, on which he is inhaling distractedly, or while pretending to be distracted by the impenetrable book. My father's face is almost expressionless, half-covered by his open hand and distorted by the inhaling on the cigarette, but even so I can see an undisguised pride, a pleasure at acting the model, at seeing his son trying, comically, to imitate him. How little they have in common now, I silently exclaim, excepting only the blue eyes that confuse so many people. At what moment did my brother decide to distinguish himself from that man, to stop seeing himself in that face, to abandon his gestures and habits?

Maybe my brother always had his own way of going about his activism, that's what I think straight afterwards, in an unreasonable attempt to reconcile their similarities. The anecdote that comes to mind now is a simple and expressive one: it happens on one of the many afternoons when my father is out, my mother is home, shut away with a patient in the room that served as a consulting room. It's possible that this circumstance alone would be enough to trouble such a young boy, but it's worth adding that my sister had been born a few months earlier, and I suppose this might have increased my brother's uneasiness still further – albeit the photos with the baby show him to be quite affectionate. The anecdote is as trivial and as opaque as any story worth telling. It happens on a silent afternoon: my brother opens the door to the consulting room and, saying nothing, without invading the forbidden space, without trying to aim at either his psychoanalyst-mother or the patient rendered speechless by his act, hurls a big Argentinian apple as hard as he can, the apple splattering on the parquet floor.

My parents enjoy telling this story; I always enjoy hearing it. Then I ask, not sure why I need to, whether they ever found out what it was that was upsetting the boy, what his militant behaviour was about, why he was acting up – if there, in this place where their struggle was drawing to a close, my brother was perhaps starting his own. He never explained much, you know, one of them answers quietly. Your brother always preferred actions to words. So I continue my meditation on the possible difficulties in handling a child who barely resembles them at all, on the conflicts that may arise when faced with such unpredictability, such instability, the constant disrupting of expectations, the power of surprise. In time my father interrupts me: you think your brother is the only one who's different from us, unpredictable, unstable? You think any child ever allows himself to be moulded? Our children always transcend how we think of them. Not one of you was ever what we imagined, not one of you matched what was expected of you, and that's always where the charm of it was to be found.

36.

There's an epilogue to my parents' political history, or what is conventionally called their political history – the stubborn militancy, the combative actions, the participation in collective movements. I could say, not without a certain melancholy, that there's an epilogue to their non-conformism, to my parents' rebellion against a system defined by others. An epilogue which, at the same time, might perhaps be the start of the process that would make them into the peaceful people I know today, devoted professionals, committed heads of family, adults who sit down at the table every night and patiently stir the tea in their cups.

This episode, which has something of an ending about it, must have happened at the start of the 1980s, the family of five having been formed at last, no longer living in secrecy, officially settled in Brazil thanks to the daughter who was born there and gave them their permanence. A happy family, as anybody might deduce, resembling all happy families, but still visited by feelings of exile, a cold wind bringing them distant pains, whispering stories in their ears of a horror with no end in sight. But whispers also brought the unexpected summons, murmured on the quiet by a few comrades, voices that insisted one after another that nobody could carry on like that, so calm and indifferent, that it was time to get back together, that something needed to be done and the person had now appeared who could lead them.

They met in the Água Branca Park, as determined by an ethereal voice, a voice that incited the others and whose origin almost nobody knew. The way my parents tell it, each in their own way, that prospect had made them very uneasy, they were back to the old anxiety that their Brazilian wellbeing seemed to have diluted, something of the fervour of participating in the present, of no longer ignoring its extensive ruin. They met at daybreak in the Água Branca Park, gathered beneath a rubber tree, ten or twelve people with trembling legs and apprehensive expressions. Then one man raised himself up above the group with indisputable authority and started to talk urgently about the urgency of acting, of striking the final blow against those military bastards, bringing them down at all costs with a major attack, words he strung together with no emphasis as he stuck his arm inside his rucksack, as he pulled something like a grenade out into the breaking morning light. The workings of a grenade are simple, his voice became business-like, it's just a matter of pulling this pin at the exact moment, activating the fuse, which detonates the explosive charge, all this, of course, after you have thrown it far away from you with a steady hand. So be discreet and careful as you handle it, feel its shape and texture, feel the weight of the powder, calculate the strength necessary to throw it a safe distance, the furthest possible distance.

My mother with a grenade in her hands, my mother as I cannot conceive of her, she couldn't help feeling how ludicrous it all was, how far it went against her principles, how this sinister object burned against her skin. My father, receiving that weight from her hands, hearing her whisper angrily that this was ridiculous, noticing that she was ready to leave, knew at that moment that all he wanted was to go with her, that there was nothing left to be done there. The movement had lost its way, they ranted as they walked away from the park with some relief, they still rant today when they recall it. The meaning of the struggle was being corrupted by this, by this warmongering, this irresponsibility, this fatalism. Did they want revolution, those guys, or just some company for committing suicide?

No, my parents' political history has no epilogue. The outlines of their non-conformism are more discreet and at the same time clearer: their militancy always manifested itself in a habit of questioning, challenging, arguing. The way they seem to me now, I don't feel so very different, or at this moment I do not wish to be. As I describe it now, without fiction to carry it away, the weapon once again loses any fascination. I am with my parents as they leave the park, I leave behind what I never knew. Let insubordination be limited to the reflective act, that's fine, at the living room table I take a gulp of the tea I've stirred and stirred. I would never want to hold a weapon in my hands, and saying that is itself also a form of action, it too forms part of a political history.

37.

I am with my parents at the living room table, I look at their faces wavering between surrender and disquiet, I see the usual defeat in my sister's shoulders. I don't even know how many hours the four of us have been sitting at the table, talking about my brother, how many hours this week, this month, this year, I don't even know how long it's been happening, when talking about my brother became this vertigo, this daily act, this unavoidable fact of life. What could possibly still be left to say about his distance, his starvation, his resistance, his life lived out in solitude, a life interrupted by paralysis and silence. And how much longer can we concern ourselves with his occasional movements, his sudden appearances, his intemperate exits into a city that is the very antithesis of his bedroom, a city where he performs his bursts of unruliness ever more energetically. Where he goes when he does go out we don't know, or with whom, what he does, where he loses himself. When he comes back, he shuts himself away in his room and leaves us advancing our flimsy theories, he's enduring some distant suffering he does not recognise, he's running away from his family because of undefined feelings of rage, because he's crashing into some non-existent barrier, because he doesn't want to face up to our difference. Or maybe we are the ones who can't bear his otherness, who can't understand it, who have never managed to learn who he is, and all these insistent words of ours are the precarious fruit of this inadequacy, a useless distraction, an exercise in complacency, a compensation for the more precise and fairer words we are unable to say to him. Or that's not it, somebody dissents, we shouldn't be so self-critical, maybe we talk about him so much as a desperate gesture of affection, because we want to have him among us even though he's absent. Maybe, someone else agrees. Maybe it would be good for him to start seeing an analyst, one of us always suggests, and then the others bring up an observation that has long been familiar to us all, that he won't agree, he's never going to agree. Taking him to a therapist against his will is no use, besides being an act of violence. Together we recall, with no need to interrupt the momentary silence, that distant period in his adolescence, those long years when he did see an analyst, when little or no progress was made despite such effort, despite such expectation. And the analyst calling my parents in for a conversation and being surprised at the missing information, the adoption, something so important, no, he never mentioned it, how could he have spent so many years in analysis with this glaring omission, how could he have spoken openly about himself, for so many years, without mentioning a thing like that? And so we return, and the thing is he shuts himself away, he's shut up inside his room, he's shut up in himself, and it seems there's no point trying to get close to him, it just makes him angrier, as if just knocking on his door and saying good morning were an invasion, as if somebody wanted to deprive him of the isolation he's created for himself and in which he finds his relief, his consolation, his forgetting, whatever it is that keeps him alive, the unavoidable fact of his existence.

And then, early one morning, while we're all solemnly asleep, having perhaps forgotten his absence at last, my brother arrives from wherever he had been and crashes the car hard into the pavement outside the house, into the fence, into the house. I don't know if anybody hears anything, I don't know how light my brother's footsteps are as he sneaks off to bed without anyone seeing him. It's only later in the morning, when I wake up, that I learn what has happened. He's never crashed before, my mother says. It was nothing serious, the house is fine, the car just got its front a bit smashed up, my brother's only asleep, but is it really right to say that everything's OK? Crashing into his own house: how could you not recognise that anger, how could you help but hear such a thunderous cry?

38.

They're like those mornings when we used to share a bedroom, I think, they're like the way I invent those mornings in my memory, a constant oscillation between silence and error, between embarrassment and trepidation. That's what they're like, the family therapy sessions, which are so recent and yet so easily forgotten – it's striking that so soon afterwards I already can't remember them, that they demand of me such an effort of imagination, that I am so suspicious of what I have to tell. They're family therapy sessions, no more than that: seventy-five minutes we spent each week in the same room, watched by a spectral stranger, exchanging inhibited glances and poorly-thought-through phrases. Seventy-five minutes in which we spoke so much, in which we kept so silent, afraid of saying and afraid of not saying what is essential.

A diversion, a subterfuge, had led us there. If he didn't agree to individual therapy, one of us suspected, maybe he'd be willing to go with us, maybe he'd start to get engaged with the process and stop wanting to escape, maybe soon we could disappear and leave him talking by himself. It was with these good intentions that we deceived him, I wanted to believe, though still not knowing, still not understanding, that we were only deceiving ourselves. It was for us, that therapy, it was between us that something was starting, or that something was breaking, we were the ones who needed to challenge our resistance, our immobility, our selective mutism. And because we were ignorant, because we still didn't know, we ended up drifting into irrelevant ruminations, into digressive remarks, postponing – as much as we could – any gesture from him, any pronouncement, however aware we were of the armchair to which he had withdrawn – the furthest from the sofa where we were sitting, the closest to the man listening to us.

That was when my brother expressed himself as we never could have imagined. I don't remember the words he said, words that were less important than the effect they produced. I remember that, as he talked, as he enumerated an infinity of small hurts, of upsets visited upon him from day to day, as he retrieved with growing bitterness the many mistakes we had made, the many reprehensible distractions, my father always so busy with work, my mother consumed by patients' stresses and the demands of the daily routine, my sister submerged in her paediatrics residency, me bestowing all my attention upon some book or other, I remember that, as my brother made the absurd accusation that nobody ever listened to him, nobody worried about him, nobody wanted to know if he was OK, if on the other side of the door, or of the house, or of the city, he was surviving, I remember that, as he talked, something in me was being restored to meaning. His words were fairer than mine: in his words, what he was in himself began to merge into the us upon which I so insisted, an us so partial and imperfect, an us that excluded him. There, listening to my brother get worked up under the neutral gaze of a stranger, I remember being seized by an old feeling, I remember feeling that we were *en famille*.

39.

How could he not have known we were there, my mother gets annoyed now, or my father gets annoyed now, that we were always there and attentive on the other side of the door, that for a few minutes every morning we were all pure expectation, waiting nervously for him to come out and mentally rehearsing the words we'd say to him, the precise tone of each word, the wave of a hand asking him for a kiss, the sensitive warmth of the welcome. It's obvious that not all the words we ever say to him are going to be gentle ones, my mother points out, my father points out, sometimes a raised voice is called for, a harsher note, especially when you see a child who's so removed, so sorrowful, so subdued. Especially when you sense that the child's existence is being consumed in an inescapable void, and it looks like that same void is consuming us, infecting us. Especially when we're overcome by our own impotence and it feels like no effort will ever be enough, it's never been enough, none of us has ever been enough, and we're visited by this frustration, this failure that is so very eloquent – I no longer even know who says that.

But every child is a going concern, wasn't that how Winnicott defined it? No child is dependent on his parents for waking up, and walking, and coming out of his room, and giving himself over to life. There's a vital spark in every child, says Winnicott or the analyst: something is in motion in that being who exists only for himself, something is in motion and neither father nor mother are responsible for this. Of course, parents do have a role to play in creating a healthy environment, providing what is necessary, offering stimuli, but it's perhaps worth understanding once and for all that their commitments end there, and not every problem has an error at its origin. Not everything is so simple that it involves a guilt, guilt whose expiation the two of you will never achieve. It's fictitious, suggests the analyst, or maybe it ought to be fictitious, this emptiness you feel, this frustration, this impotence, this harsh sense of your own inadequacy. After all, what fundamental mistake could you possibly have made, for him to end up like this?

And then I'm the one to take the risk, or it's my sister who takes the risk, bringing up what had momentarily been forgotten, the fact of our brother being adopted, having been adopted, being an adoptive child. What I'm trying to say, or what my sister's trying to say, is that maybe my parents feel this way because of having so actively taken on, one day long ago, the explicit task of being responsible for him, of guaranteeing that that boy would be OK, and now, unsure if they've achieved it, they allow themselves to be too discouraged by this, or they let themselves be overcome by this concern, by this desire to move him even if he doesn't want to move. But I never get around to saying it, I haven't enough breath for those words, or enough time, because the moment I start speaking, my brother is the one who grows indignant, no, it's nothing to do with that, he interrupts me harshly, what's that got to do with anything, it's got nothing to do with it, nothing to do with it, he says over and over until his message is lost, confused, reversed.

40.

There is a story in the family about an earlier adoption, a story that arises now as though we'd always known it, as though it were a part of the great repertoire that happens to belong to us. It's my mother who starts telling it, mildly, though more than mildness what her voice seems to convey is a kind of restraint, perhaps an unusual carefulness, a prudent attention to the words and ideas that might undermine her.

A long time ago, my great-grandfather had a daughter who died young – a daughter with the same name as my mother, as she points out, with some acknowledgement of the strangeness of this but not pausing to examine the coincidence, not really questioning what peculiar relationship it might have established between the two of them. To mitigate the pain of the loss, he adopted another girl, and gave her a different name, but tried to raise her with the same reference points, the same remote lineage, the same myth of a specific origin, an idyllic conception, a perfect birth. To save her from who knows what, my great-grandfather ended up never revealing to the girl the narrative that had brought her there, he ended up never telling her that she was an adopted child. Eighteen years passed before the moment of discovery, the eighteen years that so often pass in legends, until a confused event that changed everything, something like a journey to Europe and the requiring of a document. The girl was eighteen years old when she discovered what she'd been deprived of her whole life. As it draws to an end, the story accelerates, as if speed might lessen its weight: with no scandal, with absolutely no confrontation, the girl married her first suitor, left home and never came back, disappearing without a word.

I listen to this story with scant interest, not wanting to understand it at first. There's a moral that one might easily deduce from it, another of the many examples of ineptitude from which we suffer, of the inability to accept the many forms a family can take, to accept that families do not all follow the same model. Later I think I understand something more intimate: that this ancestral event, this crooked fate, this sad outcome, is something from which my parents always wanted to protect my brother, or always wanted to protect themselves. From early on they made an effort to tell him who he was, where he came from, they avoided unforeseen doubts, risky discoveries. From early on they were careful to give him what he wanted, to assure him of a full welcome, to guard against anything that might be upsetting. Even then they weren't able to save themselves, because they never could, from the possibility of an untimely flight, from the greater distance he decided to inflict upon them, from a new disappearance. And for a moment I wonder, even though I should not, even though I don't want to do them an injustice, even though I keep quiet and leave the session in silence, whether this unlimited presence of their son, this proximity inside the door, might actually suit my parents. How much his immobility, his unchanging dependence, protects them from an old suspicion, from a mythic fear. How much the battle they're now fighting in their son's name isn't in fact a battle against themselves.

41.

Someone recalls, I don't know if it's my mother, if it's my father, if it's the analyst, but someone recalls that Winnicott had an adopted son. Not an adopted son, somebody else corrects them, something like an adopted son, a boy who was in his care for a time, a refugee war orphan who had trouble adapting to his new place of shelter. What Winnicott talks about when he describes him is hatred: though delightful at some moments, the boy is ungovernable and aggressive, a constant source of exasperation, the boy makes the couple's life hell. He spends his days in an unconscious search for his lost parents, that's Winnicott's interpretation, he rejects the affection of anyone who takes him in, subjecting the new environment to constant testing. The hatred doesn't only come from the boy, hatred has overtaken him too, that's what the provisional father notices, and it's precisely this intense aversion that the boy wants to witness. Only when he sees this hatred for himself will he be able to trust the love that his new parents have to offer, will he know that the relationship that exists there is not common charity or benevolence. When he finally understands, this man turned father, the boy's need to let his feelings out, he refuses to accept the boy's lawlessness, he punishes his behaviour, he goes further still: he throws the kid out of the house and orders him not to come back until he knows how to behave himself properly. The eviction is repeated several times, at night, in the rain, in winter; the boy always comes back, each time more attached to the family, each time more a son.

What the story represents, removed from its context, is likewise not easily clarified. Nobody is saying the situation is as extreme, nobody is advocating such brutality, nobody is defending this outdated paternal strictness – my mother, my father, the analyst, whoever it was that brought up the parable is now struggling to make themselves understood. Nor are they suggesting that what my brother is feeling is hatred, or what he's suffering from is the absence of some woman, of some man, of whoever those two people were who conceived him – nobody is suggesting this nor the opposite, that his reclusiveness is a refusal to look for those people. The only idea that's being supported here is the need to oppose the son whenever it seems appropriate, to reject his rejection, refuse his refusal, deny his denial of a life together. All that's being considered here is whether there might not have been, before the first indefinable retreat, an opposite retreat: whether it was my brother who shut himself in his room, or if it was we who shut ourselves in the rest of the house, in the rest of the world, in some place that was not his bedroom. To get him out of there, somebody concludes from the midst of a prolonged silence, we would have to knock on his door, and go inside there first.

Had I heard what that somebody said or am I hearing it for the first time now? Did I need to isolate myself in this old city, did I need to start writing these old stories, in order finally to hear my father's voice, what my mother had to say, her acute doubt, her shrewd uncertainty? Having been expelled from my brother's room so many years ago, why have I never known how to go back to it? Why am I taking so many nights, so many rains, so many winters, to go back and knock on his door again, to make myself more of a brother to my brother, to hug him just once more? Why have I never been able to forget, why have I wanted to seek refuge so far away, and in whose name, to whose benefit, out of hatred for whom, in search of whom?

42.

You all talk too much, you all talk too much and you don't see.

What a powerful transformation can take place in somebody's mind, what an intense process can happen behind an impassive expression, vacant eyes, a neutral face. In a body which in every respect is an incarnation of indifference, in a body empty of any words or gestures, in a body so forcibly emptied, there is often something that feeds itself, something that is free to grow in silence. Something none of us knew about, something we weren't able to recognise in time. None of us noticed his growing impatience, none of us spotted in his trembling fingers the counting of the days, the apprehensiveness with which my brother awaited each new restrained conversation, each new controversy, each session of therapy.

You all talk too much, you talk too much and you don't see, that was the accusation he made one morning when we could barely see one another, one morning when each of us was getting ready to follow our own pre-determined paths. We were at the table having our morning coffee when he hurled his unexpected accusation at us, like somebody hurling a grenade or an Argentinian apple, like somebody who for a long time has needed to be heard. Within moments we were all in his bedroom at last, occupying the whole space that was forbidden to us, leaning on the wall, on the bed, on the desk, stunned by his euphoria, following or trying to follow this unprecedented outpouring of words, so copious that they paralysed us, numbed us. You all know or pretend you know so much but you don't understand. You don't understand what it's like living so horribly alone like this, it's so ridiculous being this alone when you're being surrounded, supported, pursued. You don't know what it's like being paralysed like this, feeling like everybody's got someplace to go while I stay here, in the same place I always am but still lost anyway, standing behind the door, with the key in my hand, but unable to open it. You can't imagine what it's like, being repelled by the door, attracted to that enormous window, that enormous pane of glass, that balcony, what it's like leaning off that balcony after a day of total emptiness, what it's like hearing something from the ground calling out to you, what it's like to feel that vertigo. You don't know what it's like going out at night, finally managing to go out after all this endless anxiety, what it's like to ask for something strong, feel the impact of that strength and keep on going, ask for that thing again and keep going, you don't know what it's like to want to destroy yourself.

These were not the words, I don't really know what words they were, but this was what my brother was saying, more agitated than we'd ever seen him, unable to decide on any particular place in his room, on any position, on a focus for his restless gaze, his uncontained outburst. You all worry, I know you do, and you get upset, but you're only upset for a minute and then it passes, it lasts an hour and then it passes, you get distracted and go on with your lives. There was one day, a long time ago, he was talking to my sister and me now, his eyes had forgotten their rage now and become sad, one day you got distracted, you went on with your lives and left me alone here. We'd been together up till then, one day we were all together and the next it was everyone for themselves – literature, medicine, any excuse would do.

You can't understand what it's like. It's like somebody's sticking a needle in your vein that feels like it goes on for ever. It's been thirty years someone's been forcing that needle into your skin, it's been more than thirty years someone's been sticking that needle into your vein without you noticing, you just feel the pain and don't know where it's coming from. And even when you do notice, when you do finally see, there's no use trying to pull that needle out because it's a part of your arm now, and there's a fear that's growing bigger and bigger that someone else will show up and want to pull out the needle, and they'll end up ripping off a part of your body. And while my brother slapped his forearm with his hand, the skin a little redder with each blow, while I tried to understand what it was, that needle, who that somebody was who was sticking a needle into him, what substance was emptying into his vein, who the other person was who would rip his arm off with such violence, while I did my best to decipher all those things I didn't understand and was never going to understand, my brother spoke the words I would be unable to forget, the words that brought me here: that's something you should write about one day, about being adopted. Someone needs to write about that.

We didn't go out that evening, but we didn't go back to the bedroom, and my brother didn't go back to the bedroom either, we all stayed in the living room while he gathered his close friends, with such urgency in his voice that almost all of them showed up very quickly. I just wanted to tell you all I'm adopted, my brother explained with a mixture of solemnity and grief, his voice subtly overcome, an inexplicable shame he was unable to hide. Maybe I shouldn't trust my memory so much, maybe the impression I have is false, but I remember that on this occasion there was no boasting or awkwardness, there were no hidden glances, no unnecessary anxieties. So what?, asked the first, spreading his hands palm-up and shrugging. What difference does that make?, added another bluntly. We've known a long time, but who cares? We've never cared about that at all, said a third who was already getting up to leave.

Was it relief my brother felt as he watched them go, or was it just tiredness? If it was tiredness, its origins must have long preceded the events of that day, coming from well before that verbal storm – an ancestral tiredness. That night, though he was exhausted, though the euphoria had given way to an inexorable exhaustion, my brother didn't want to sleep in his bedroom. We put a mattress beside my bed, he lay down and for a long time I noticed he didn't close his eyes, and his eyes had nothing vacant about them, I thought, they were the glassy surface of liquid depths. When I woke up, in the middle of the night, I felt a touch on my body: it was my brother's arm reaching out from one mattress to the other, it was his hand resting on my chest.

43.

Rereading my account of that episode, that climax in our story, I briefly regret having forgotten to mention the tears: as if describing how much we cried while my brother exploded into speech might change the meaning of everything, or might increase its intensity. Then I pull myself together and find myself asking why I'm so interested in tears, why I'm so keen to resort to this easy means of drama. Why am I attracted to a voice that wavers, why do I love eyelids welling up, eyes moistening, if my whole life I've battled against this inevitable overflowing, against excesses of affect, against fragility. But an adult who cries is not weak, that's something I've learned with some conviction, that's a lesson that no longer eludes me: an adult who cries without shame is a person of an enviable transparency. I wonder then whether it mightn't be a product of this envy, the attention I pay to the sad stories, to the devastating scenes, and my disregard for what is joyful and tender in our vast relationship.

And yet there isn't much that's joyful about the event that returns to my memory now. I was four or five years old, swinging the hammock my brother's lying in. Higher, he says, and I climb onto a low wall to fulfil his wishes. Higher, he insists, and I try so forcefully to push the heavy fabric that I end up swaying and falling, and crashing onto the harsh cement floor. It's only from my brother's shrill shout and his flailing run towards me that I understand the seriousness of the fall, a moment later I find myself surrounded, my uncle takes me up in his arms and we're on our way to hospital. My forearm is broken in two, that's what the doctor says or my uncle, and the two parts need to be fitted back together quickly. Since I had lunch not long ago it's best for me not to have an anaesthetic, the pain will be bad but it'll pass quickly, it's just one more jolt to my arm. Now it's my sharp cries that fill the walls and hallways, but soon the pain does pass, I calm down, and I see the pride on my uncle's face.

He didn't cry a single tear, my uncle says when we get home, as he will say again whenever he remembers that afternoon, whenever he wants to please me. Shortly afterwards I learned, because my sister told me secretly, likewise very proud, that my brother cried while I was in the hospital, that my brother felt guilty or remorseful and tearfully confessed, that my brother suffered so badly for me that he needed to be comforted. And now I understand why this episode has arisen from some unfathomable corner, emerged from the vast expanse of my memories and images, interrupting the story: that night it was me who wanted to sleep next to him, I put my mattress next to his, and on his chest I rested my other arm.

44.

I walk the streets of Buenos Aires, I look at the indistinguishable sequence of façades, I look at the names of the streets. Belgrano, Sarandí, Carlos Calvo, I walk without being able to get my bearings, I trace square loops around the grid city. I'm lost, but it takes me a while to accept that I'm lost, it takes me a while to accept that I'm able to get lost amidst such topographical rigour. If I'm lost and I keep going round in circles in such a logical city, I muse as I walk, it's because I don't want to arrive at a central point, it's because I resist reaching the destination I've chosen, it's because I'm trying to escape whatever's waiting for me when I get there.

Then I spot the street sign for Virrey Cevallos and at last I can pick up the pace. I realise I have found my way when I notice I'm not alone, I'm walking in the company of other agile legs. A small crowd is gathering at the headquarters of the Grandmothers of the Plaza de Mayo, I spot the excited waving of their arms from some distance away, I feel their shouts vibrating in my thorax. With some effort I clear a path between the bodies, but I soon tire and let myself be swallowed up by the throng, I let my body become one more element in the mass – though I hadn't noticed the cold before, I appreciate the heat of community now. I'm no longer trying to reach the door, I'm standing a few metres from the entrance, and on some comrade's radio the news that has brought us together is repeated: today they are announcing the finding of one more grandchild. It's only grandchild number 114, four hundred grandchildren are still missing, four hundred children snatched away after birth, four hundred unknown destinies. It's only grandchild number 114, shouts the emotional announcer, but this case has a particular symbolic value, it's the grandson of Estela de Carlotto, the long-time leader of the Grandmothers. It's been thirty years, more than thirty years of searching, of waiting, of fighting and tenacity, more than thirty years culminating in this afternoon.

On a makeshift screen in the window the image of a lady appears, pinkish skin around her deep eyes, her smile broad and frank, her white hair in disarray, the woman starts to speak and the silence that's imposed is instant. In a voice that sounds unexpectedly firm, she is celebrating the great joy that life is granting her, the extremely long battle won, a well-deserved victory for justice and truth. Her family is complete today, or nearly: the vacant chair he'll soon be able to occupy, the empty picture frames that have waited so long for him will now contain his image. I've already been able to see what he looks like, he's beautiful, the lady says without changing her tone of voice, without a pause before any of her words, her peaceful face framed by the serious suits of the people supporting her. He's beautiful and he came to find me, what we grandmothers have been saying has been fulfilled: they will come looking for us. We don't know the whole story, we'll have to piece that together. But this is for all those who say, enough, for those who still doubt our struggle. For those who want us to forget, to turn the page as though nothing had happened. This is reparation, yes, for him, for me, but also for the whole of society. Except it's not full reparation: we need to keep looking for those who are missing, other grandmothers need to feel what I'm feeling today. In any case, thank you: all I wanted was not to have to die without holding him in my arms.

When the crowd becomes a whirlwind of shouting and clapping, I realise I have no choice but to shout and clap, I realise I cannot restrain my hands or my lips. Somebody at the back calls up the memory of all the disappeared, of all those imprisoned, and together we raise up the usual chant, together we assert that they are and will be present, now and always – *presentes, ahora y siempre*. There's a kind of ecstasy in what we're experiencing here, there's a euphoria that runs from shoulder to shoulder, that is sensed from mind to mind, there's a collective frenzy nobody could have predicted. On the radio the announcer is doing his best to define what has happened, this eloquent chapter in our national history, this belated triumph against terror and forgetting, this happy outcome contrary to all expectation, this feeling of a country being reconciled.

When we have stopped shouting, when there are no longer any voices to be heard, when the crowd around me has dispersed and I notice that once again I am walking alone, I feel as though not much of that euphoria remains in me. I'm happy, I've fulfilled my wish to be there, to follow this event from up close, to contribute my presence and my solidarity and lose myself among others. I'm happy for them, but there's an unease in my happiness, in my chest that's now empty of shouts there's a slight melancholy. I couldn't get into the headquarters of the Grandmothers, I was left outside watching what was going on, and the regret that washes over me now feels like something more than just a whim. Hearing the silence of the streets, swallowing the cold air, I'm no longer deluded by the collective exhortation: even if I show up here, even if I make myself a ghost walking its corners, I'm absent and I'll always be absent from the country's reconciliation, I'll always be a distant admirer of Argentinian events.

And then I understand, or think I understand, why I turned a distant fear into a solemn fantasy. Then I understand why I so wanted to find the Grandmothers, why I exiled myself to their main headquarters, why I visit their sacred sites, their museums and memorials. Why I study their stories so tenaciously, why I scrutinise the faces of their daughters, why I insist on a probable lie, against all evidence, the idea of my brother as a disappeared grandson. This wouldn't give his life meaning, as I once suspected. This wouldn't absolve him of his distressing immobility, of his empty present. It's me, not him, who wants to find a meaning, it's me who wants to redeem my own immobility, it's me who wants to go back to belonging to the place where I've never actually belonged. Finally understanding, finally located – I decide, finally, to leave: nothing will restore me to anywhere, nothing will repair what I have experienced, because it doesn't look like there's anything in me to be repaired.

45.

How immeasurable is the time of inaction, the time of distance, the time of silence, how different it is from this other time of meeting, of voices overlapping, of faces seeing one another. I cross the city with my sister beside me, once again I see the landscape I left behind, I'm surprised to find I appreciate the dirty river that runs alongside us, and I think about none of this, I reflect on none of it, consider none of it. The time of meeting encourages an abandoning of ideas, it's made of pure matter, thin fingers holding the steering wheel, lips unveiling teeth. I cross the city with my sister beside me and surrender myself to the pleasure of company, I hear the latest stories that she tells enthusiastically, I marvel at the exuberance of her days, the profusion of occurrences. I reciprocate cautiously, I again thank her for her kindness in coming to meet me, I tell her vaguely about the period of time that's drawing to an end, I eclipse my long experience of Buenos Aires behind banal comments about existence.

About the new house they bought on impulse, about the confusion of the increasingly complicated renovation works, about her patients' constant state of disturbance, everything in her speech suggests a continuity, an expansive present, a life proceeding. They want to have another child before long. Miguelito is already three years old, he's practically a teenager, she jokes and straight away laughs, he says whatever comes into his head, he invents stuff and I don't know where he gets it from. It's amazing how like you he is, she tells me, physically, I mean, he's sort of got your manner, the way you go red when you're nervous or embarrassed, something about the way he concentrates when he's playing with his toys, and the way he'll devote himself to any book, too. Then she talks about our brother, who's an uncle now, you should see what he's like with his nephew, how free he becomes, he spends hours having fun with the boy, squeezing his cheeks, teaching him things I never would have known, it's amazing, there's something in him that relaxes.

For a moment I can't find an answer, I lose the thread of her comments, the conversation breaks up into static silence and I revert to introspection, to the obsessive examining of my feelings. I think I've neglected my sister, that I've grown distracted from what's been happening to her, that by giving in to other chimeras I have abandoned her too. Talking about the family, I think as the car crosses the grey city, writing about the family and reflecting so much on it isn't the same as experiencing it, sharing its routine, inhabiting its present. I think about time: if I don't know my family, if I have so little sense of it left, this must be an old book. I think about time: how many years did I take to write it, how many months did I isolate myself, how long since the stories have been different, since the conflicts have dissolved?

46.

We meet around the same table, there are five of us in that pronoun, it's already past nine o'clock and we're still talking. For now, we don't return to the serious old stories, our conversation has been circling around minor daily anecdotes, joking about small annoyances, testing the vibrations of our voices to see if we recognise one another, if we are acquainted. I notice that, after so many years, we have become more Brazilian, or more alien from what we once were: dessert now is the fruits that are colouring our plates, not the hands gesticulating lightly, not the nimble words we scatter around us.

It's only when my siblings leave, only when we've already moved on to the second cup of tea, that the tone of the gathering turns more serious. The previous night my parents had read the book I sent them, they cheated insomnia with these pages, they spent some time perfecting what they might say, how to deal with this somewhat bizarre situation. Obviously they can't make merely literary observations, both of them point out as if wanting to say sorry, the whole time they were reading they felt a weird duplicity, they felt torn between readers and characters, oscillating endlessly between history and story. It's strange, says my mother, you say mother and I see my face, you say that I say something and I hear my voice, but very soon the face is transformed and the voice is distorted, very soon I can no longer recognise myself. I don't know if that woman is me, I feel like I'm represented and yet I don't feel that way, I don't know if those parents are us.

There's always a sad tinge to your writing, she goes on and I notice a sense of hurt. I understand how attached you feel to intensity, but I'm not sure I understand why it's all got to be so melancholy. You don't lie the way writers usually lie, and yet a lie is constructed all the same; I don't know, maybe I'm just trying to defend myself by what I'm saying, but I suspect we weren't like that, I think we were better parents. We did struggle with your brother a little, it's true, and you're faithful to the sequence of events, as faithful as it's possible to be to the instabilities of memory, but I wonder if he ever got that bad, if he was ever really so elusive, so hard to deal with, if he really was inaccessible in his bedroom for so long. I remember and I don't remember a lot of the things you describe, the harsher episodes, but your commitment to sincerity is obvious, a commitment I can't totally decipher. I didn't really understand, though, why you chose to reverse the conflict with food, subverting your brother's being overweight and portraying him as thin. But I was glad that there was at least an obvious deviation, as a suggestion of so many other deviations, I was glad that not everything is reflecting reality or trying to be its imitation.

Because my father isn't speaking, because he never interrupts her to express any discrepancy or disagreement, because he nods vaguely without paying too close attention to what she's saying, I know how rehearsed this speech is, I know they have shared out the roles, discussed at length what would be the most appropriate response. I should tell you that some inaccuracies did bother me, my father takes his place on the stage, my father takes his turn to speak. I never kept guns under the bed; I kept guns in the house, yes, but I'd never have kept them under the bed, not somewhere that obvious. And the dinner you describe so that you can later make a suggestion of torture, our friends' absence at that dinner, there's no way we would ever have been so upset. They were hard times, dinners got cancelled. What I'm trying to say is that this militant you're describing seems too naïve to me, and I don't want to recognise myself in that naïveté. And having all this discussed at the end, with us showing up to critique the book, making observations, pointing out inaccuracies, it might even be an ingenious device, but I can't say I'm sure it redeems anything.

That scene in the Água Branca Park is ridiculous, my father goes on, and now it's my mother signalling her emphatic agreement: how could anybody in broad daylight, in the middle of a park, take a grenade out of their rucksack? That passage I did think lacked plausibility, my father says, and for a moment I can't contain my annoyance: but that's how it was, you've told me, it's something I think I remember clearly, for some reason I registered that. There are a lot of peculiar things in your story, I point out, that's not the only one. I even had to miss some out because no reader would ever believe them: how could anyone accept that you'd gone back to Argentina at the height of the regime, clandestine and vulnerable, how to accept that you'd taken such a risk to try and adopt a little girl? Well, maybe, my mother tries to ease the situation, maybe so, the meeting in the park might have happened, my father agrees and concedes: those really were implausible years.

Deep down I think we're both talking about something else, we're making up obstacles, because this book bothers us a little, we have to confess, we're troubled by so much overexposure. It's my father who asks the questions: what's to be gained by such a detailed description of old scars, what's to be gained by this public scrutiny of our conflicts? If your brother had parties where he ransacked the house with so many people, if you're describing it as an invasion of our territory, what kind of ransacking are you encouraging here yourself, what invasion of the most intimate things we have? Now I say nothing, now no argument comes to my aid, but I notice my mother signalling for him to soften what he's saying, apparently rejecting the incisive approach. Openly she appeals for calm, let's not get worked up, there's no need to talk like that, nobody is sorry the book's been written.

I understand, of course, he goes on in a milder tone, that there's a lot of working through of everything we've experienced, that the book's another kind of therapy, it's where an emotional story gets filled out. But in this case, shouldn't it be kept between us, a text for us to read together, and interpret, and discuss? I know, we know, that it's a book totally infused with care, loaded with affection, I know the ambiguity isn't limited to us, that the book itself also has ambiguity in every line. There are moments, though, when I catch myself doubting, I'm not sure it should exist so openly. I just don't want you to act on what I'm saying, I've never wanted that: keep on going, Sebastián, you've done what you had to do, and you never know, someone might even find a good novel to read in there.

47.

I am and I'm not the man who walks down the corridor, I feel and don't feel the weight of those legs moving beneath me, I hear and don't hear the noise of those feet against the floor. In my body's indelible memory, do I still retain the boy who hesitated so many times, the boy I once was, or am I only the man who arrives at the door and decisively raises his closed fist? It lasts no time at all, almost no time at all, the knock, it's just the banal banging of four fingers against a piece of wood, and yet, there is an extensive past that echoes within them, the long day of anxieties and indecisions. I am and I'm not standing outside my brother's bedroom, holding and not holding a sheaf of pages under my arm, I don't really know what I'm doing here, if I want his embrace, if I want his forgiveness.

I wait and while I wait I'm assailed by an unfathomable fear. I don't really know what question I'm asking, I can't find quite the right words for that fear, but I think I feel an old insecurity assailing me, I think I'm asking whether these pages might really be worth anything. Would the book I've managed be good enough, would the possible book be sincere enough, would it be sensitive enough? Am I, with this object, answering his old request, am I handing over exactly what my brother once wanted, or have I distorted any desire of his too much, have I merely invented his wish in order to make myself more lyrical? And then, when the footsteps I hear on the other side of the door light up new beacons in my fear, it's no longer the book I'm worried about, I no longer care about the book. Suddenly it's me, child or adult, who is making himself the object of scrutiny, I'm the one who has to respond to the discreet echoes of time. And then I no longer know if I've been sufficient, if I've been the possible brother, if I've been good enough, if I've been sincere, if I've been sensitive.

My brother opens the door and doesn't give me any answers: in his presence, the questions fade away. My brother is a solid body positioned in profile, he's an arm held out to invite me in, he's a bedroom I'm surprised to find so peaceful. He isn't wearing a shirt, and his torso is neither fat nor thin, his scar now no more than a wide trace that I make myself seek out. I notice I'm avoiding his eyes, I don't want to look at them. I enter the room head down, and it's as if I am occupying it, as if there's no space for anything else; I notice that there is no space in the room for words. In a few moments I'll give him the book, and maybe then the words will find their place. For the time being, yes, I do finally just look at my brother now, I lift my head and my brother is there, I open my eyes properly and my brother is there, I want to get to know my brother, I want to see what I have never been able to see before.

The epigraph by Ernesto Sábato was reproduced with the
generous permission of Schavelzon Graham Literary Agency.

CHARCO PRESS

Director & Editor: Carolina Orloff
Director: Samuel McDowell

www.charcopress.com

Resistance was published on
80gsm Munken Premium Cream paper.

The text was designed using Bembo 11.5 and ITC Galliard.

Printed in July 2019 by TJ International
Padstow, Cornwall, PL28 8RW

Printed using responsibly sourced paper and environmentally
friendly adhesive

MIX
Paper from
responsible sources
FSC
www.fsc.org   FSC® C013056